13
haunting tales

Edited by Terri Karsten
Illustrated by Kayla Fayerweather

WAGONBRIDGE PUBLISHING

Winona, MN 2013

Wagonbridge Publishing
661 E. Howard
Winona, MN 55987-4302 U.S.A
Orders at Wagonbridge Publishing: wagonbridgepublishing.com

First Edition Softcover
ISBN-10: 0982855230
ISBN-13: 978-0-9828552-3-2

This book is published as a work of fiction. The publisher makes no claim regarding the veracity of the tales herein. There is no proof ghosts exist. Only stories. As for truth, that's for the reader to decide.

Table of Contents

ịnтroduꞓтịoꞑ

You might expect them in cemeteries, but really they're everywhere. Ghosts lurk in the cracks and crevices of our homes, basements and attics. They hover about the fringes of a campfire, and haunt the lonely crossroads on the edge of town. You can find them in the long empty hallways of a dorm or in the dark alleys of the city. Old manor houses with creaking steps and banging shutters house legions of ghosts and it's a rare castle that doesn't claim at least one such spirit. Even newer places like office buildings or hospitals might attract a ghost or two.

Around the globe, belief in ghosts is widespread if varied. From the bamboo forests and riverbanks of China, to the steppes mountains of Europe, and to the tundra of the far north, stories of spirits of those who died and came back to haunt or help the living abound. These spirits of the dead can be benign or even helpful as in the cartoon of *Casper the Friendly Ghost,* or the spirits might be truly evil, as malevolent as those found in *The Amityville Horror.*

Superstitions and stories about ghosts come from all over. Certain times seem to attract ghosts, like All Hallows Eve or Halloween. October 31, the eve of All Saints' Day, is known also as Samhain, the Celtic New Year, when the barrier between our world and the world of spirits is open further than usual. Dry, skittering leaves, bare branches and chill winds of the season add to the creepiness and lend credence to the stories, but fall is not the only time ghosts wander the earth.

In China, the time for ghostly hauntings is thought to be late summer. People may burn ghost money to keep the spirits away. Since many Asian ghosts inhabit water, it is advised never to swim in lakes or oceans in the ghost month, or the ghosts will drown you. Whistling or hanging out clothes at night are also ill advised since both activities might attract vengeful ghosts. It is always a good idea to knock on any hotel room doors at this time before entering,

5

in order to give fair warning to any ghosts that might be lingering inside.

Meanwhile, in Benin in West Africa, January is the month for the Voodoo Festival, based on the religion of the Yoruba people. The festival's religious ceremonies include dancing, snake handling, and sacrifices made to keep ancestors and other spirits at rest.

Just as many different cultures believe in ghosts, there are many different ways ghosts can appear. In North America ghosts are usually white or translucent spirits, shrouded in tattered rags. Think of children draped in white sheets for Halloween, their ghostly giggles flitting from house to house. In other places ghosts may be dripping with seaweed, or they may show up as eerie lights called will o' wisps or ghost candles. They haunt the marshes and lead travelers to a watery death. In parts of western Europe and North America, many people believe seas birds like gulls and petrels house the ghosts of sailors who drowned. Ravens are also thought to be able cross from the land of the living to the land of the dead, carrying the spirits of those no longer living. In Thailand, ghosts may appear as dead humans, or they may be seen as monsters. Hungry Thai ghosts with sharp teeth might even turn an ordinary person into a cannibal.

With so many variations on the theme, it's no wonder that so many people have a story about a ghostly encounter. In the modern world, it's great fun to tell ghost stories around a campfire, and almost everyone knows someone who claims to have seen a ghost, or at least to have heard a story about someone who knows someone who has seen a ghost. In my search for original ghost stories, many people had their own personal encounters to relate.

When I was staying at the lighthouse on St. Helene in Lake Michigan, we spent one evening telling ghost stories around the campfire. One woman told about a teenage friend of hers who had an illicit rendezvous with her boyfriend near a lonely section of railroad tracks. The teenager said she and her friend passed a man with a lantern as they walked back into the woods, but when they turned around he had vanished.

Other visitors to the lighthouse talked about a little boy

haunting the light tower. That night eerie whistling and singing echoed down the spiral iron staircase. But in the morning three pranksters confessed to the "haunting."

One place in Winona well -known for its ghosts is Pieces of the Past, now a furniture and decorating store. Since it was built in the 1800's, the building has been a bar, a law office and a brothel. The current owners, employees and customers all claim to have seen, heard or felt many of the former inhabitants. Owner Cheri Peterson pointed out that a lot of different folks have worked in the building and a common thread among them was they didn't like going in the basement. One story she told was about a bartender from the 70's. He sent a couple of workers to the basement to bring up a heavy case of liquor. The two guys started down the stairs, but suddenly they stopped. They looked at each other wide-eyed and wary, but neither one said anything.

When they came back upstairs, one of the guys suggested they each write down what they saw on the steps and compare notes.

Both wrote "lady in a pink dress" and claimed they had passed her on the stairs. It turns out that the building has been the scene of several murders. One obituary of a woman murdered there a hundred years ago closes with how nice the poor woman looked in her pink dress. Coincidence? Perhaps. Perhaps not.

Others in the building have talked to a young girl, maybe 9 or 10 years old, named Carol. Some people working alone in the basement claim that they felt her pull on their pants like a mischievous child seeking attention.

All of these ghosts, says Cheri Peterson, are more mischievous than scary. They play pranks like chiming the bell when no one is there or rearranging the décor in the store overnight, but more than one person has felt a creepy chill in the back room or the basement. And, Cheri says, the ghosts always become more active after she's been talking about them.

One of the best stories I've heard is from my friend, Mike Halloran. On a vacation a few years ago, he visited Kronborg with his wife and daughters. Kronborg is also known as Elsinore, the castle in Shakespeare's play, *Hamlet* and the site of the Hamlet's famous encounter with his ghostly father. Mike hung out in the chapel for a few hours while his family toured the castle.

While he was waiting, Mike made friends with the docent, a retired colonel who, because of his French language skills, was adjutant to the Queen. They had a good time cracking jokes in English and French, and talking about the long history of the castle and how the story of Hamlet actually occurred a couple hundred years before the castle was built.

When a pair of English tourists walked in, the docent winked at Mike and said, "The English all ask the same question."

With that, he walked over to them and started telling about the chapel and the castle.

"Pardon me," the woman interrupted. "Do you ever see ghosts?"

The docent stood at full attention, and looked her straight in the eye. "Madam, in the 300 years I have been working here, not once!"

The stories in this collection range from the serious and scary to the light-hearted and whimsical. Each ghostly encounter offers a different idea of what haunting means. The best way to read them? By flickering candlelight, of course, with a cup of hot chocolate close by.

Devil's Creek

by Paul Maitrejean

The tension of waiting for her engine to die again almost made Erika miss the tiny green sign that said, "Devil's Creek: Pop. 119."

"Great," she muttered.

Her return trip from researching the logging industry in northern Wisconsin had gone well up until ten miles back, when her Taurus started running funny and finally died on her. A little engine CPR, as her friend Sean had called it when he coached her over the phone, had gotten it limping along again, but it still needed immediate attention. A look at the map showed a tiny dot marked as "Devil's Creek." Judging by the population, the odds of finding a mechanic here didn't look so fantastic. Her hopes plummeted.

As the wooden bridge rumbled under her tires, she got a quick glimpse of the village. A narrow main street cut through a one-church-and-two-bars town, a conglomeration of trailer homes and poorly constructed buildings. No sign of a garage anywhere. Plus, one of the biggest, blackest storm systems Erika had ever seen towered over the pine woods to the west, blotting out the setting sun. The weather forecast predicted severe thunderstorms for the whole night. If she didn't find a mechanic and a place to hole up in Devil's Creek, the next twelve hours would be interesting.

She entered the town and pulled into a small gravel parking lot, where the wind kicked up sheets of dust and shook the volleyball net on the far side. Half a dozen pickup trucks and small cars stood in front of a steel-sided building marked as a bar only by the electric Coors sign hanging in the front window. In a small town, the best source of information was the local taproom.

Cigarette smoke burned her nostrils the moment she walked in. A small radio blared the latest Brooks and Dunn hit. Eight or nine men, all of them in work clothes, sat at the bar, twisting around to study the newcomer. Two others paused in their game of pool, looking her up and down. A teenage boy stood playing a pinball machine, from which emanated some of the most annoying sounds Erika had ever heard.

"Get somethin' for ya?" The tall bartender spoke in a loud voice accustomed to yelling. Erika guessed from his build that he also fulfilled the role of bouncer when necessary.

She smiled. "No, thanks. I was just wondering if you had a garage in town. I'm having car problems."

One of the guys at the bar shook his head. "Nah. Not a real one, anyhow."

"Car problems?" A lanky man in overalls and a John Deere cap stood up, a can of MGD in his hand. "What kind of problems?"

"I'm not sure. A friend of mine said it might be the alternator."

"What make?"

"Ford Taurus."

The man grinned. "I think we can help you. Hey, Verlo!"

The kid at the pinball machine glanced up. "What?"

"C'mere."

The boy abandoned his game and approached. Erika noticed dark smudges on his face. Long blond hair hung over his eyes. He wore a black shirt with the words: "This Is The Shirt I Wear When I Don't Give A Crap."

"This here's my son Verlo." The man slapped the boy on the back. "The kid's thirteen, but he can fix anything on the planet."

"Something broke?" Verlo asked. Puberty played havoc on his voice.

"This lady says she's got a Taurus with a bad alternator. Ready to make a few bucks?"

Verlo grinned. "Sure!"

"All right. Let's go take a look." He gave Erika a triumphant smile.

Erika fought down a wave of dismay.

Verlo and his father – whose name, he revealed, was Axel Krass – led Erika and her unwilling vehicle to a cluttered outbuilding about a block away from the bar. A lime green doublewide trailer home stood beside the building. Axel moved a lawn tractor and a wheelbarrow with three dead raccoons in it, making room for the Taurus. Once inside, Verlo got her to pop the hood.

She stood in the shed's doorway, watching the storm blow in while Verlo tinkered.

Devil's Creek lay strangely quiet. Few lights shone in the windows. Nobody walked around outside. Compounded with the rising wind moaning through the evergreens and the grumble of approaching thunder, the quiet struck Erika as eerie.

"Well, it's your alternator, all right." Axel stepped beside her, wiping grease off his hands with a dirty rag. "She's on her last leg. But that's okay. We got a junkyard on the other side of town. I remember a Taurus gettin' hauled in there just this spring. We can take the alternator out of it." He paused. "Providing mice haven't gotten at the wiring yet."

"Looks like the town's bunkering in," Erika said. "Expecting a humdinger of a storm?"

Axel nodded. "Of course, the legends make it worse."

She gave him a curious look.

He tossed the rag inside and smiled. "It's just a bunch of superstitious horse manure. They say the Angel of Death visits Devil's Creek every seventy years. And according to old Fillmore Schwartz, tomorrow will be the anniversary of the last visit. Seventy years to the day. He says this storm is a har . . . har . . . har-something-or-other . . . like a messenger to say the Angel is on his way."

"Harbinger?"

Axel snapped his fingers. "Yeah, that's the word he used. Harbinger."

"Every seventy years, huh?"

"Yep. The legend goes all the way back to when Indians had a little village right here, before the white man came. Like I said, though, it's all nonsense."

A deep rushing sound eased into their conversation – a distant, muffled roar that approached like a speeding train. Erika looked to the west. The stormclouds roiled overhead, a deep churning black that grew even more ominous as the sun vanished for the night.

Over the trees, a heavy grey sheet blotted out all the storm's features and moved in on Devil's Creek at an intimidating pace.

"Here she comes," Axel said.

The storm hit like a hammer. Rain crashed down in undulating waves, blown in a wind that tore small branches off the tossing trees and carried them away. Lightning lit the rain, turning each drop into tiny points of falling fire.

"Shoot." Verlo slammed the hood and came to stand beside Axel. "We ain't getting to the junkyard in this."

"Not tonight, we aren't." Axel shrugged. "Oh, well. We needed the rain."

Erika sighed. "Looks like I'm staying in Devil's Creek tonight. Where's a good place to crash?"

"Marlys over at the café has an upstairs room she rents out," Verlo said. "Thirty bucks a night, and you get breakfast free."

"Good coffee, too," Axel said.

Erika opened her trunk and pulled out her suitcase and an umbrella. "Looks like that's where I'm headed, then." She locked her car. "How long do you think this rain will last?"

"A couple hours, easy," Axel said. "Maybe longer. Fillmore Schwartz says the one seventy years ago lasted nearly twenty-four hours. Flooding and the works." He shrugged. "But that's only if you believe the old fart."

The accumulated smell of years' worth of breakfasts permeated the Devil's Creek Café as Erika stumbled through the door, a little jangling bell announcing her entry. She dripped with water. The wind had caught her umbrella and tried to yank it away, and she'd spent more time wrestling the umbrella than keeping it between herself and the rain. She shook her head and pushed strands of sopped red hair away from her face.

"You look like you need a cup of coffee."

Erika blinked water out of her eyes. A scrawny weathered woman in Levis and an apron stood holding a broom in one hand, taking in her drenched customer.

"That sounds really good."

The woman gestured to a coat rack near the door. "Leave your stuff there and come take a stool. I've got a fresh pot on right now."

Erika dumped her suitcase and hung her umbrella and rain coat on the wooden pegs. When she reached the counter, a steaming cup of coffee waited for her.

"Thanks." She sat down and took a grateful sip. She looked up at the woman. "Are you Marlys?"

"Uh-huh." Marlys wiped the counter with a damp rag.

"Good. They say you've got a room I can rent for the night."

"You heard right. Comes along with breakfast, too." Marlys studied her. "I've never seen you before. Where you from?"

"A little east of La Crosse."

Marlys leaned on the counter with folded arms. "Then I'm guessing the storm forced you into Devil's Creek. Nobody drives all the way from the other end of the state just to come here."

"Actually, car trouble. Axel Krass is helping me."

"If you want to live, young lady, I suggest you leave immediately."

The voice came from behind. Startled, Erika turned.

An old man sat in a corner booth, a half-eaten sandwich on a plate before him. He looked at her with light grey eyes, his bony fingers holding a glass of iced tea. Lighting flashed in the rain-battered window behind him.

Marlys gave an exasperated sigh. "Oh, for Pete's sake, Fillmore. Give it a rest."

"I mean it." The old man raised an eyebrow. "She'd best leave town."

Erika looked at him for a moment. "Is this about the Angel of Death legend?"

He set his iced tea on the table. "You've heard of it?"

"A little."

"Tonight is exactly seventy years from the last time the Angel came to Devil's Creek." He spoke with the precision of education. "He's returning tonight. He never comes for the old or the sickly. He comes for somebody healthy. Somebody who by rights shouldn't die."

"Why?"

An expression of suppressed anger flickered across Fillmore's aged face. "Because he's a thief. That's what he does. He steals souls. Souls to which he has no right."

Erika picked up her coffee and left the counter. She slid into the booth, across the table from the old man. "Were you here when he came last time?"

"I certainly was. I saw him myself."

"Tell me about it."

"There's little to tell. A storm much like this rose, and lasted until the next morning. At the time, the only way out of town was across the bridge, but the flood washed it out. He came at dark and walked up and down the street. Nobody escaped town. Something always happened to stop them. The storm was the worst any here had ever seen."

"What did he look like?"

"He wore a black robe or cloak with a hood, much like what medieval monks wore a thousand years ago. He walked through the storm easily, because the storm was his." He leaned forward, his voice lowering. "But I got a look at his face."

Erika nursed her coffee, letting it warm her. "And?"

"I was a young man at the time. I had my eye on a pretty girl who lived on the end of this street. While most of the townsfolk stayed in the church and prayed, her father refused to believe that the Angel of Death had come. So he kept his family in their house. But I decided to go see her, the storm be damned." He took a sip of iced tea before continuing. "I nearly ran into him head on. I saw into his hood." Fillmore stared out the window, remembering. The lightning cast eerie shadows over his crags and wrinkles. "He had a dead face, as pale as ashes. His mouth was a crossways slash. His eyes were black empty spaces." He sat back again, returning his attention to Erika. "I thought surely he would kill me. I stood still, terrified. I stared at him, and he looked at me. Then he walked away."

"Who did he take?"

"Maribeth. My girl." His jaw tightened. "He stole her, and my ambitions and dreams along with her." He pondered for a few moments, then picked up his sandwich. "He's coming back tonight.

Anyone in this town is open game for him."

He took a bite out of his sandwich. Erika watched his wizened mouth work, and a tiny coldness seeped into the center of her chest.

The signal icon of her cell phone's LCD display showed no bars. Erika held the phone high, tried various corners of her tiny rented room above the café. Nothing. She'd truly stumbled upon Podunk, Wisconsin.

She turned off her cell and stuffed it back into her suitcase, then pulled out her laptop. Nothing stopped her from work, anyway. She brought up the word processing program, kicked back on the creaky bed, and wrote.

Al Markam walks the length of a massive pine log, measuring it. He shoots a spot of yellow spray paint on the log's end. "Logging is a struggling industry now," he says –

A crack of thunder blasted overhead, startling her. The small lamp beside her bed flickered.

Erika set her computer aside and walked to the window, where she could look up and down the main drag. Rain still fell in massive volumes. Water rushed down the street in small, manic rapids and poured from overtaxed gutters. Rain spouts exploded their contents like hoses. Tree branches lay scattered everywhere. Trees whipped about as if trying to uproot themselves.

If this kept up much longer, Fillmore Schwartz's prognostication of flood would become reality, if it hadn't already.

She started to turn away, but a motion outside caught her attention. She paused and squinted, bringing her face close to the glass.

The steel awning over the window, while groaning and rattling in the wind, still kept the torrents of rain from obliterating her view. In the direction of the bridge, where occasional cars stood parked on either side of the main drag, somebody walked along the middle of the street, into the wind. Erika watched in disbelief. Who in their right mind would try to walk outside in weather like this?

The wind shifted, sending rain sluicing across the panes. Her view blurred.

The figure now appeared as a smudge through the rain rattling against the glass, moving steadily down the street. The streetlights flickered. Lightning flashed, the blazing white glare throwing the walker's shadow in a long streak of black.

Then, just as the person came directly before the café, they turned and moved toward the front door.

Lightning washed out Erika's vision. Thunder sizzled and cracked in a deafening roar that shook the building.

The lights blinked out.

Downstairs, Marlys pierced the storm's chaos with a shrill scream.

Erika's blood stopped cold. Fillmore's story rushed back in a wash of chilling realization.

Had the Angel of Death come to the Devil's Creek Café to claim Marlys?

Nonsense. She shook her head to banish the superstitious stories. Something had happened to Marlys, and she had to find out what.

A quick search through her suitcase dug up her little keychain flashlight. She clicked it on and stepped into the hallway.

Lightning cut the blackness, white knives stabbing through the windows. At the end of the hallway, the stairway gaped like a black mouth. Erika felt her way toward it, one hand on the wall. At the head of the stairs, she shone her light down. The steps descended to a landing, then turned right to the first floor.

"Marlys?"

Thunder covered her voice, crashing overhead.

Erika started down. The creaking of the steps blended with the rain and wind beating against the building. With each step, Erika's pulse beat harder. While the storm's noise covered her own approach, it also camouflaged any sounds an intruder might create below. Did someone wait for her at the stairs' foot? She didn't dare imagine it. Right now, Marlys needed her.

At the landing, Erika bent down to see into the café. In the nearly constant flicker and blaze of lightning, the room appeared deserted.

"Marlys?"

A tall hooded figure stepped before the foot of the stairs, not ten feet away, a black silhouette against the lightning.

Erika staggered backward, her scream catching in her throat. She tripped and fell against the wall, landing in an awkward sitting position.

She stabbed with her flashlight as if it were a weapon.

The beam fell on the features of Axel Krass peering out at her from the depths of his raincoat.

Relief flooded over Erika. She let out a huge sigh and let her head drop forward. "Good grief, Axel! You scared the living daylights out of me."

"Sorry. You okay? Looked like you hit the wall kinda hard there."

"I'm fine." Erika stood up. "But what about Marlys? I heard her scream."

Axel nodded. "Yeah, I heard it when I come in. The power went out just as I stepped through the door. Ain't found her yet."

"Let's look around."

Axel made way for her, and she entered the café, shining her light around.

"Remembered I'd left my chainsaw out in the woods this afternoon," Axel said. "I headed out on the road west, then this big old tree keeled over, right onto my truck. Another foot and it would have crunched the cab. I came walkin' back, and thought I'd stop here for a rest. That storm is hellacious. Pulls the breath right outa you."

Erika only half listened to Axel. Her spot of light played around the room. She checked behind the counter, then in the kitchen. Nothing.

Axel called, "Here! I found her!"

She rushed back into the dining area. Axel stooped behind a table, standing over Marlys.

The café owner lay on her back, staring at the ceiling with wide eyes.

"Is she hurt?" Erika knelt beside Marlys.

"I dunno." Axel studied the prostrate woman. "She don't seem like it. She's alive."

Marlys shifted her eyes toward Erika, and her lips moved. Erika leaned closer, bringing her ear within inches of Marlys's mouth.

"The . . . gel . . . deh . . . Angela . . . deh . . ."

My God." Erika looked up at Axel. "I think she's having a stroke."

Axel frowned. "You sure?"

"Not really, but we'd better not take any chances. Call an ambulance."

"Right." Axel dashed for the kitchen, rubber boots thumping against the hardwood.

Marlys raised a feeble hand, finger extending toward the door. ". . . gel . . . death . . . here . . ."

"The Angel of Death?"

Marlys gave a weak nod.

Everything fell together now. The power going out, just in time for the hooded Axel to appear in the café door with the lightning behind him, had scared Marlys into a massive stroke.

Despite her ridicule of Fillmore Schwartz's story, she'd believed it enough for an unwitting Axel to literally frighten her nearly to death.

"Phone's dead." Axel returned, an edge of panic in his voice. "Is she gonna die?"

"She might, if we don't get her to a hospital pronto."

He grimaced. "Nearest hospital's twenty miles away. But your car's busted." His tone turned sour. "And mine's scrunched under a big ol' tree."

"Then we'll have to borrow one."

"Marlys keeps hers out back." Axel hurried to the door. "I'll go get it."

Erika could barely see through the windshield of Marlys' '89 Cutlass Ciera, despite the wipers' frantic pace. Beside her, Axel hunched over the wheel, peering hard at what little of the road he could see. Marlys lay wrapped in a blanket on the back seat.

The huge tree that had smashed Axel's truck blocked the road west, and Axel said for a fact the bridge over Devil's Creek to the east had already washed out. So now they drove on the remaining route out of town, a narrow southbound road. In the insane blaze of lightning, Erika saw the tossing evergreens on either side, looming like giants that wanted to stoop down and sweep the car away.

The tires cut through at least an inch of water. Erika didn't know if the rain fell that hard or if the terrain had flooded that much. Either case boded little good.

"You really think I scared her coming in like that?" Axel almost had to shout over the rain pounding on the car.

"It's the only explanation that makes any sense," Erika said.

"Man." Axel shook his head. "I feel real bad about that."

"There's no way you could have known the power would go out at that exact moment. It was just poor timing. It's not your fault."

Axel considered for a moment, then nodded. His jaw thrust forward. "No. It ain't my fault. It's that stupid old coot Fillmore Schwartz's fault. He's the one who's been running around town filling folks' heads with that Angel of Death hogwash. If it hadn't been for that, Marlys wouldn't have been so on edge to start with."

Probably true, Erika thought, but she didn't say it. No need to get him worked up now. "I think he believes it, though."

"Sure he does. But there's some things you just don't run around telling people, no matter how much you believe it. I mean, say you were nuts enough to believe in ghosts. Go ahead and believe it. It's your right. But there's no cause to tell everybody and their brother that you see dead people. Next thing you know, you've got a bunch of other loonies seeing ghosts in every corner, and what have you got? A town full of folks like Marlys, just waiting for nothing to scare 'em into the hospital."

"You're probably right," Erika said. She peered at the rain slashing across the windshield.

And saw a band of blackness just ahead.

"Look out!"

Axel hit the brakes with both feet, bracing against the steering wheel. The vehicle fishtailed. The resistance of the road under the car's tires vanished, and the Cutlass hydroplaned.

Water sprayed against the undercarriage with a hoarse roar.

The headlights revealed a gully chewing its way across the road, wild water churning through it. Asphalt clung to its rim in ragged chunks.

Axel swore. "Hang on!"

At the last moment, the tires gripped pavement. Rubber squealed. The car slowed with a jerk, then slammed down as the front wheels slipped over the gully's edge. The car ground to a halt. The violent water rushed by only inches away from the headlights.

Axel gripped the steering wheel with both hands. He stared at the trap that had almost swallowed them, and whistled. "Holy buckets! That was just a little stream this morning. Must have wiped out the culvert and everything." He looked over at Erika. "You okay?"

She nodded, unable to talk much with her heart pounding like a manic boombox. She glanced into the back. Marlys still lay on the seat, strapped in with the safety belts.

Axel shifted the car into reverse. The engine revved. The front wheels spun, throwing rooster tails of water, but the car didn't budge.

"She's stuck." Axel swore again and slammed his fist on the wheel. "And in this ungodly weather."

"What should we do?" Erika asked. "Wait it out?"

"Heck, no. We're no more than half a mile outside town. We can hike back."

Erika almost laughed. "Are you kidding? In this? What about Marlys?"

"I'll carry Marlys. I'll wrap her in my rain coat and put her on my back."

She shook her head. "I still think we should sit this out."

"Well, a stranded car ain't no place for a woman with a stroke. Besides, the water ain't gonna stop rising. And Verlo won't like being alone at home for long. He hasn't been taking that too well since his mom left." He paused. "Matter of fact, my place is closer than the café. We'll just head back there."

Erika took a deep breath and tightened her damp jacket around herself. The storm's roar reminded her of a jet engine. She nodded. "Okay. But let's go fast."

Axel handed her his rain coat, and she clambered into the back to unbuckle the safety belts and maneuver it onto the mumbling woman.

"Ready?" Axel said.

"Yeah."

Axel killed the engine and doused the headlights. Darkness pounced on them, broken by the constant stutter of lightning. He hopped out and opened the back door. With Erika shoving and Axel pulling, they maneuvered Marlys onto his back, limp arms draped over his shoulders.

Erika had to stand behind her to keep her from slipping off. Rain hammered them in smothering waves.

She handed her flashlight to Axel and turned to slam the door shut.

A tall figure, cloaked and hooded, stood on the opposite side of the gully, silhouetted in the lightning. Erika stared. A sensation such as she had never experienced before – a slow, sinking feeling, as if a frozen lake drew her into its black belly – twisted her stomach. She clutched the car door so hard the edge dug into her fingers.

"Axel!" she finally shouted over the wind and thunder. "Look!"

He turned.

A pause in the lightning threw them into utter darkness for a moment. When it resumed, the ominous shadow had vanished.

"What?" Axel squinted through the rainwater running down his face. "I don't see nothin'. C'mon!"

Erika managed to unclamp her fingers and close the door, but she scanned the road and the woods, hands raised over her eyes to shield them from the rain, trying to find the mysterious stranger.

"Hurry it up!" Axel shouted. "This ain't sightseein' weather!"

Erika followed him up the road, one hand on Marlys' back, but she continually looked behind.

The coldness in her chest told her, without a doubt, that she had seen something supernatural. Something that made her take the legend of Devil's Creek far more seriously.

Erika staggered through the door of Axel's trailer house, gasping for air as if she'd fought her way through a lake, rather than rain. Water plastered her hair to her head and face. Her jacket hadn't prevented water from penetrating to her skin. Her wet clothes weighed her down like sandbags. Helping Axel carry Marlys across the doublewide to a worn sofa took all her energy.

A high-watt flashlight beam descended on them. "Dad?"

Axel pulled his raincoat off Marlys and turned. "Yeah, it's me, son."

"You sure took a long time," Verlo eyed Marlys with curiosity.

"I know. Sorry about that. I'll explain in a minute." He turned to Erika, who straightened Marlys out on the sofa. "I got some clothes my ex left here, if you want 'em."

"That would be great. Thanks."

Axel hurried into an adjoining room. "Verlo, get a towel for Marlys. But don't bug her. She's not doing good."

Verlo stood beside Erika. "What's wrong with her?"

"She's had a stroke. Hurry up and get that towel. She doesn't need to catch a cold on top of everything."

Verlo hurried off.

Erika knelt beside the sofa and buried her face in her hands. Her heart still pounded. She fought to calm herself, to even her breathing. Even so, the incident on the road stuck in her head.

Her mind fixated on the silent, hooded figure she had seen. Had it really been there? Or had her overstimulated emotions somehow conjured it up?

And if it had been real, then had it truly been the Angel of Death? Who was the Angel after? Had he come for Marlys? Or had he come for Axel – or herself?

"Here we go." Axel returned wearing dry clothes. He handed her a bundle – a pair of blue jeans and a checked blouse. "The bathroom's just past the kitchen if you want to change there."

"Thanks." Erika took the clothes and stood. "Is there anyone in town who knows something about first aid? We need to know what to do for Marlys until we can get her out of here."

Axel considered, then shook his head. "Robyn Newgate was an RN, but she moved to Iowa last year. Don't think there's anyone else in Devil's Creek who'd know."

Erika gave a heavy sigh of helplessness. "Then we can just make her comfortable."

Erika lay in the recliner beside the sofa, watching the incessant rain and lightning through the window across the trailer. Axel and Verlo had both gone to bed two hours ago, leaving Erika to keep vigil over Marlys, who now lay sleeping. Axel had offered her the use of his bed, but she'd elected to sleep in the living room.

She shifted, pulling the light comforter closer. Her nerves, the strange surroundings, the isolation, and the vicious storm refused to let her sleep. Fillmore Schwartz had said the storm would last all night. If so, Marlys would have to go without medical attention for six hours more. Anything could happen in that time. She also wondered about her animals at home. Sean had promised to take care of them, and probably checked in tonight. He'd likely tried to call her. She could only imagine what he was thinking right now – maybe guessing that she'd had an accident.

She hoped he wouldn't call the State Police. That was the last thing she wanted.

Erika slipped out of the recliner to check on Marlys. The moment her stockinged feet touched the carpet, sharp cold drove into her center like a chilled spike. She halted. An inch at a time, she turned, looking around the trailer in the lightning's blue-white glare.

Nobody.

She eased to the center of the doublewide, where she could see down the short hallway.

At the very end, Verlo's bedroom door stood open.

Her fear shot higher. She wanted to run into a corner and hide until everything had passed. But a nagging worry kept her from following her instincts: Verlo.

Fillmore Schwartz had said the Angel of Death never came for the old or sick, but for those who, by rights, should not die. Verlo, a hearty youth in his early teens, fit that description.

She couldn't, in good conscience, not check on him at the very least.

She forced her feet forward. Her instincts screamed at her to run, to hide, to leave this house. To leave Devil's Creek. Her heartbeat pounded in her ears.

Step by step, she walked down the hallway, until she stood a few feet from Verlo's bedroom door. She looked in.

The twin-sized bed stood against the far wall. A long mound raised the covers where the boy lay sleeping despite the pounding storm. Erika almost breathed out in relief. But the sensation of dread remained. Something still wasn't right.

Was Verlo dead?

Her first impulse was to wake Axel, but she didn't want to look like a fool if her apprehensions proved false. After a few moments' hesitation, she advanced into Verlo's bedroom.

Lightning blazed through the windows, shredding the darkness like an insane strobe. Erika found herself blinded alternately by brilliance and darkness. Somehow, the experience was worse in this room than in the rest of the house.

Gradually, her eyes adjusted.

The tall figure in the corner remained still, a shapeless mass that blended with the shadows. Even before Erika realized it was there, she stopped. The whole room pulsated with deep forboding that turned her joints soft. She stared at it, praying it wasn't what she thought it was, and knowing it was anyway. She held still, like a rabbit freezes when it senses danger, with the crazy notion that the threat would fail to notice her and pass on.

She watched the apparition, for how long, she didn't know.

Then a tense whisper crept out of her mouth. "Why are you here?"

No answer.

She couldn't bring herself to repeat the question, too afraid to speak further and knowing she had been heard the first time. Whether it answered or not was its own prerogative. Without speaking a word or moving an inch, it had established with sheer presence who controlled the situation. Erika, not the Angel, was the intruder here.

Besides, the question was ridiculous. She knew why he was here. Why else would the Angel of Death be standing in this room? But still, why? Why Verlo? Why an innocent boy?

The Angel moved out of the shadows toward Verlo's bed, with no perceptible walking action, as if he glided a bare inch above the floor. She saw the black cloak that hid his entire figure. A deep hood kept his face – if he had one – hidden in darkness. He stood over Verlo, bending over him as if studying the slumbering youth.

Erika wanted to step forward, to reach out in protest, but the cold terror kept her welded to the spot. Her voice came as the barest squeak:

"Why him?"

The Angel straightened. The hood turned toward her.

"Why?" she repeated. Her tongue felt glued to the roof of her mouth. "What has he done?"

Without sound, the Angel spoke.

She heard no words either with her ears or in her head. He just looked at her, and she understood the empty blackness within the hood as if reading the expression on a face.

The Angel had come to take Verlo, not because of something he had done – but because of something he would do.

Thoughts of future events paraded through Erika's mind. She didn't see them actually playing out, but rather knew of them in the way she knew of things she read in a newspaper. She was remembering – only remembering something that had yet to happen.

Verlo, now a boy of only thirteen, would grow up to become a vicious killer. Nine women and five children would die horrible deaths at his hands. They would die by means of a hunting knife that, at this moment, lay in a box under Verlo's bed. He would scatter their dismembered corpses all over the state. The hunt for their killer would last years, involving the best crime detection experts available, but in the end he would elude capture. Verlo Krass would never face justice.

Erika reeled under the shock, a mental blow that almost overwhelmed her terror at standing not ten feet from the Angel of Death himself. Verlo . . . a psychopathic murderer . . .

The Angel had come, not to arbitrarily deal out death, but to save lives.

The Angel's mission was not one of terror and destruction, but of order and preservation.

Erika stepped back, even more scared of getting in the way. Not only would she be interfering with a supernatural being, but she would also be trying to allow unspeakable acts to play out in the future. But still . . . she couldn't get past Verlo's youth. Though she now knew what sort of adult he would become, her eyes still saw a boy sleeping in his bed, blond hair splayed out around his head like a halo.

The Angel watched her for a while, as if deciding whether she would try to stop him, then turned back to Verlo. He stood over the bed for a long time. Then he leaned forward. One arm, long sleeve draping off it like a curtain, reached toward the boy. Erika saw a finger extend, long, narrow, like a distorted skeleton's.

Erika turned away and closed her eyes. She couldn't watch . . .

A hurried step from behind startled her, and she opened her eyes again, turning.

An old man, stooped, dripping rain, his thin white hair clinging to his head like spiderweb, glared past her at the apparition in Verlo's room.

"Stop!" Fillmore Schwartz's voice snapped like a firecracker amid the rumbling thunder.

The Angel of Death lifted his finger from the boy's forehead and straightened, facing Fillmore.

"I saw you coming here." The old man raised a shaky fist. "I saw you coming, and I won't let you do it again! You stole Maribeth Nelson from me. She should have been mine. She was mine! I won't let you steal another soul. Not again."

The Angel of Death remained tall and silent, a black silhouette against the lightning. With a slow turn of the dark hood, he looked down at Verlo, then back at Fillmore.

Erika also looked, and drew in her breath.

Verlo lay in his bed as if still asleep, eyes closed.

But somehow, even from across the room, Erika knew he no longer breathed.

28

The Angel stepped back into the shadows.

"No!" Fillmore rushed to the bed, felt Verlo's neck for a pulse. Then he whirled. "NO! Not again! Not again!"

But the Angel was gone.

Fillmore screamed his rage at the ceiling.

Erika remained frozen in the doorway.

Morning arrived clear and quiet. Aside from the puddles, the flooded creek, and the scattered debris, one would never have guessed at the previous night's chaos.

Axel, devastated at the sudden and inexplicable loss of his son, mourned in his trailer house. The locals cut away the tree that had fallen across the westbound road and pulled Axel's crushed pickup aside so someone could drive out for help. Verlo's death left many of the Devil's Creek residents scratching their heads, but others only nodded in the near-smugness of having been right all along.

An ambulance arrived within the hour to carry Marlys away.

Since the grieving Axel was in no condition to complete the work on Erika's car, she paid one of his neighbors to locate the replacement alternator in the junkyard and install it in her car. Her revived Taurus now stood parked outside the Devil's Creek Café with her suitcase in the trunk. She had just opened the door, poised to get in.

Fillmore Schwartz sat on the café steps, watching a group of men clear branches and trash off the street. His grey eyes peered out from under the brim of his battered felt hat. His fists lay clenched in his lap. "He always does things that way. He always takes someone who shouldn't go. Someone with a future. He's a thief. A thief in the night."

Erika started to tell him of what the Angel had revealed to her in Verlo's room last night, but decided against it. How would she relate it without sounding completely insane? Also, she realized, if Verlo had been taken because of deeds he had not yet committed, what did that mean for Maribeth, Fillmore's old love? Fillmore would never believe her. So she chose to say nothing on the matter.

"I'm sorry your first taste of Devil's Creek was so poor," Fillmore said. "It's really a nice little town. You should come back sometime."

An electronic ring from her purse made Erika jump. She pulled out her cell phone. Miracle of miracles – she'd finally found a signal. The caller ID read SEAN. She said goodbye to Fillmore and got into the car.

"Thank God," Sean said when she answered. "Are you okay? I've been calling you all night."

"I'm fine." She pulled into the street and rolled westward. "I got stranded in a little town called Devil's Creek. I'm just leaving now."

"Devil's Creek? My dad and I hunted up there once. We ate at the café a couple of times, but there was this old guy who hung out there that gave me the creeps."

Erika hesitated, then launched a guess. "Fillmore Schwartz?"

"Come to think of it, that was his name. How did you know?"

"I met him."

"Holy cow – really?" Sean laughed in disbelief. "That guy must have been ninety when I was there thirteen years ago."

"He gave you the creeps?"

"Good grief, yes. He was always complaining about how something had been stolen from him. But you know what really got me?"

"What?"

"I asked him what was stolen from him, and he looks me right in the eye and says, 'A soul. But I just got a replacement.' Bizarre, huh?"

A slow coldness slid across Erika's flesh. "Thirteen years ago?"

"Yeah, about that. Why?"

"That . . ." Erika's voice caught. "That was when Verlo Krass was born. Oh my God . . ."

"What?" Even over the phone, Sean sounded puzzled. "What's wrong? Who's Verlo Krass?"

She looked in the rearview. Fillmore Schwartz stood in the middle of the street, watching her leave. Ice sluiced through her.

"Erika?"

"I'll call you back."

She hung up, gripped the wheel with both hands, and acceler-ated, intent on escaping Devil's Creek.

canдlestick guilt

by Jordan Elizabeth Mierek

"Mother, you can't live here." I should've stopped gaping, maybe smiled, but instead sputtered forth – my mother should've never purchased the shack on Hark Street. "Your home in Davidson was perfect. A two-story house with white siding and a screened-in front porch all nestled in the village." This new place, with its weathered bricks and cracked stone stoop, crouched between a parking lot and a highway.

Mother smiled as she shut the front door. The hinges squealed the whole way, and she had to shove the door to make the latch click. That would have to be fixed before someone tried to break in. "But you're not in Davidson anymore."

Davidson was only an hour away. I glanced at my husband who picked at the hallway's peeling pink paint. Maybe we shouldn't have decided to move so soon after the wedding, but Curtisville was closer to his job.

"I can help you take care of the baby." Mother went so far as to pat my stomach. I stepped back and yanked down the hem of my red sweater.

"I'm not pregnant." My husband, Tom, and I had decided to wait a few years to get settled.

"You do want kids." She didn't leave it as a question. Still smiling, Mother strode past me into the next room, the kitchen.

"Let it go," Tom whispered.

I stuck my tongue out at him before I followed Mother. Tom's parents lived in Florida near his brother, but ever since my father had died, I'd been responsible for Mother. She would be the safest in Davidson, a quaint little village she'd lived in since childhood.

"Why did you have to choose this place?" I pointed at the faded walls. Dark spots in the orange paint revealed where pictures had been removed. Some of the tiles in the floor turned up. Other than the sink, stove, and refrigerator, the kitchen stood empty.

She patted her short bob, a few gray strands in her hair as black as mine. "It was the cheapest."

Of course. Who else would want the dump? "How old is this?" The lime green cupboards screamed 1970's, and I hadn't even been born yet in that era.

"It was built in 1901. His daughter inherited it, and lived here until she died in her sleep five years ago."

I winced, sticking my hands into the pockets of my jeans. Father had died five years ago.

"Wait." I widened my eyes. "She died in her sleep? Like, here?"

"In her bedroom, yes. Poor dear. A family member must've found her."

Mother had gone insane. "You're living in a house where someone died?"

"Awesome," Tom said from behind me. His sarcasm was just so helpful. I punched his arm to make him stop.

Mother snorted. "She isn't a ghost. Come help me unpack the U-Haul."

Two more trips with the thing and she'd have all her stuff she wanted here. The rest she planned to sell in an estate sale or donate to the Salvation Army.

"I'll help." The floorboards squeaked under Tom's feet as he headed to the driveway.

"It's a very nice house." Mother's voice softened and she clasped my hand. "You and Tom can visit anytime."

I squeezed my eyes shut and sighed. We should've never found an apartment here. It was my fault Mother had sold her house and bought this. She'd wanted it to be a "lovely" surprise. "Thanks, Mother." I had to help her make it work. She couldn't move back to Davidson without owning a home there.

While Mother went out to the U-Haul, I peered into the living room at more old orange paint and a dented hardwood floor. The bathroom tiles at least looked newer, and the porcelain was clean.

I opened the door to the cellar and switched on the light. A bulb flared in the ceiling and hummed to illuminate the narrow steps and dirt floor.

A dirt floor? Was that even legal anymore? Mold could grow down there. Cold could rise. I groaned. Tom and I would have to pay to get that cemented over – we owed Mother that much.

The bottom step creaked. Odd.

The second step up creaked, the sound rolling, as if someone had stepped on it.

The third step up creaked.

Hairs rose on my arms and my skin prickled. No way. The fourth step creaked. I clutched the doorknob as though it could keep me grounded. My lips dried. The fifth step, now. Impossible, they couldn't be creaking like that. A breeze couldn't do it. A dirt floor couldn't make it happen. I should run, slam the door.

The sixth, seventh, eighth.

"No." The word scraped from my throat.

The tenth step creaked and a rush of cold blew past me with enough force that I stumbled backwards.

"Bailey?" Tom held Mother's lamp with the bright blue shade.

"Did…you feel that?" I licked my lips. "The cold air?"

"A draft. The cellar must not be heated."

Right. Shut the door. My hand trembling, I pushed it closed. It had to have been my imagination. My anger and frustration over the new house.

"Where should I put this?" Tom patted the lamp. "It was in her old living room, right?"

"Yeah." I folded my arms to still the shivers.

Mother entered through the front door with her cardboard box of T-shirts. "Let me show you the bedrooms."

I forced myself to grin. "Can't wait!"

The hallway stairs creaked. Each moan made me wince. They sounded just like the cellar staircase, except no one had been walking there. Did the past owner still reside within the walls?

"We'll paint for you," I said to calm myself. "Any shades you want." The old house in Davidson had been blue, Mother's favorite color.

"We can pick them out together." Mother set her box in the first bedroom.

"Which one did the lady die in?" My throat felt tight, as if someone tried to choke me. I had to calm down. No point in freaking out over what had to be nothing.

"The middle bedroom. I think I'll use that for sewing." She turned the Venetian blinds on the window to open. "She lived a long life, Bailey. It was her time to go. She wasn't murdered."

"You don't think her ghost..." I trailed off, blushing. Mother wouldn't have purposefully bought a haunted house.

"Ghosts aren't real." Mother brushed dust off the blinds onto the floor carpeted with stained brown. "We'll give this place a proper cleaning. Scrub it all down with Clorox."

I leaned against the doorway. More Venetian blinds cast darkness over the middle bedroom. "Are you sure she died in that one?"

"I spoke to her daughter." Mother clicked her tongue. "How sad she didn't want to keep the place in the family, since her grandfather had built it."

I lifted my eyebrows. Of course the daughter wouldn't want to keep it. Everything needed work and the views weren't that great. Through the old windows, I could hear the vroom of traffic on the highway.

"He worked at the lumber mill," Mother continued. "Built the house for his new wife. They had four children, but the youngest passed away as a child." Her lips turned downward. "Pneumonia. He'd lost something of his father's and thought it was outside. Since his father was so angry, he went into the snow looking for it and came down sick."

I winced. "The father must've never gotten over the guilt."

"The daughter said the worst part was that her mom had hidden it on her brother as a joke. She never got over the guilt either." Mother wiped her hand on her khaki pants. "Guess I'll get the next box."

I hovered outside the middle bedroom. More pink walls and another stained carpet. The rooms were average sized. I stuck the toe of my sneaker under the carpet and worked it up an inch to peer underneath at the wood. With a little polish, we could make the room work without the ratty covering.

Movement on the upstairs landing caught the corners of my eyes. "Mother, we can—"

A little boy, around seven years old, stood at the top of the stairs. He wore a pale button-up shirt and dark pants with boots that laced around his ankles. A crimson scarf tried around his throat and a hat covered his head.

"How did you come in?" I shoved my fists into my hips. Ah, the open front door. Since the house had been empty, he'd probably played around inside.

Silent, he ran down the stairs. I jogged after him, grabbing the railing to tell him to stay out, but saw only Tom carrying one of Mother's kitchen chairs.

"Where'd the kid go?" I called. "Did he leave?"

"What kid?" Tom set the chair down.

"There was a boy up here."

Tom rubbed his forehead. "Didn't come through."

"He would've had to…" The creaking steps, the rush of air. Had I imagined the child?

Coldness nipped my skin. With a final glance at the middle bedroom, I hurried down to Tom. Stress wouldn't fool with my sanity.

A week later, I sat in Mother's new kitchen peeling paint off the walls onto open newspapers. Her footsteps sounded upstairs, interrupted whenever she switched on the vacuum. Tom cleaned out the garbage from the cellar. When the previous owner's daughter had cleared the house, she hadn't bothered to remove the broken lawn furniture or outdoor Christmas decorations.

The house could work out after all. Having Mother near would mean I wouldn't have to worry about her as much. The contractor Tom had hired confirmed the house was sturdy. With fresh paint and Mother's scrubbing, it would be livable.

"I found it," a child said from behind me.

I dropped my paint scraper and froze. It plinked against the tile floor.

My neck muscles ached as I turned only my head. The little boy I'd seen upstairs hovered beside the kitchen table, a grin on his face. He clutched a gold candlestick against his chest.

"I found it." His voice sounded hollow, as though it echoed from an empty space.

Something shimmered from the left. I twisted so fast I tumbled backwards onto my bottom.

A man in a dark suit stood near the backdoor with a grin wide enough to match the boy's. The man held out his arms and the child ran to them. Happiness and relief washed over me, so strong it made my gasp.

In the space of a blink, they vanished.

No way. What was that?

"Bailey?"

I screamed, bumping my shoulder against the wall.

Tom frowned at me from the doorway. "Bailey, you okay?"

I parted my lips, but a squeak emerged. How could I start to describe that?

Tom held up a gold candlestick, exactly like what the little boy had cradled. "Would you believe I found this in that dirt floor? A corner was poking up and I hit it with my foot."

Mother's story about the son who'd lost something and gone searching in the snow. It must've been that candlestick. He'd finally been able to return it to his father.

"Do you think anyone ever missed it?" Tom rubbed the dirt off the base with his thumb.

"Yeah," I whispered, "but it's okay now."

It would look perfect on the windowsill in the middle bedroom.

with dawn's coming

by D. R. Greyson

I am aware now, again. I lie in my bed, changed. I think it's my bed. Somehow I know that it is dark outside; the sun is fled. I cannot see clearly. There is a fog of confusion all around me. Shadows of memories tease me. Who am I? Am I alive?

I close my eyes and listen. I can hear sounds, maybe voices, coming from another room. What has happened to me? I try to think. Where am I? Is this place really my home or some other's? It feels so different to me. I am different. I try to catch one of the memories floating around me. I suddenly remember pain. A great deal of pain and hurt, a lifetime's worth of anguish stabs me and wakens me further.

I remember more. I am a warrior, or was once. Not some soldier but a true creature of the Way. I remember my former greatness. But that all changed one day. Or did it? I am so confused. I was so focused once. Alive and willful, but now I am a shadow of my former self. I remember that something terrible has happened to me, something monumental. But what?

The emotions start to waken me, burning me. Anguish, loss, fear, and pain. So much pain. Maybe even lust and...love?

I cry out. My body shakes. Or at least I think it does. My whimpers trail off but no one comes to save me. I don't want to feel anything any more, but I am in trouble. A darkness is creeping into my mind. Sadness and misery are slowly being pushed out by a building rage. Few people have truly known the fury of anguish, a nova of pain, the desperation burning your nerves from the inside, melting you. My whole body shakes and convulses with pure, unbridled hatred...at everything that has happened to me...at everyone...at myself. I know now I should have been gone long ago, but I am anchored here in the darkness by my misery and suffering. So

41

much pain. So many scars, both inside and out. I cannot leave, not yet. I am a lord of the universe! There is no man on earth like me. I have been denied, but I will not flee.

I stay there silent in the darkness, motionless. I can still hear voices from outside the room, muffled but alive. They sound unconcerned and nonchalant. I cannot hear them clearly enough to understand them. Perhaps I am in hell? They could be my demon captors guarding me here in my prison in the dark.

I rest and force myself to be motionless and calm. I cannot breathe and a drowning sensation washes over me. Calm. I must stay calm, disciplined, focused. I need self-control like I had in the days of old.

Eventually the pain lessens. I grow relaxed in the darkness. I know not for how long but a sliver of serenity finds me and I start to feel...neutral? Soon the pain is gone and I am numb again. Or dead? Perhaps I am once again a man of ice, untouched by the world? I don't feel better. I don't feel anything.

Time passes and then I rise. I realize I can see again. Soft, dim moonlight has crept into my prison from a small gap in a window. I see a door. I flow to it, sure-footed and confident again, a warrior, master of his surroundings. I turn the handle and am surprised when it opens easily, unlocked. A shaft of dim light enters my room from beyond the door. Quietly I open the door further. I see a long hall of closed doors. At the far end of the hall is a room lit by a lamp and I can hear the voices coming clearly to me from that direction.

I am barefoot and walk silently down the hall. Nothing creaks to warn of my approach. The lights and sounds grow stronger as I reach the room. A lamp shines on a table on my left. I see a television directly across the room against the wall. It is on. The voices that have enticed me are coming from people talking on some program. It looks like a game-show.

I carefully enter the room and see a long sofa against the wall on my right. It faces the television. I stop when I notice three people sitting on the sofa, none touching. At the far end in the corner of the room sits an old, seething, spiteful man. His nose is red and his eyes glazed from years of obsessive drinking. In the middle is a small, sad, blonde-haired boy. He looks so lonely and confused and his blue eyes are red from crying. Closest to me is a woman, red-haired, puffy-faced, and with a small bump on her nose. Her eyes are also red from crying. She looks miserable. None of them see me. They watch the television. Either they cannot see me or they are choosing to ignore me. At their feet lies a black German Shepherd. Only she turns to look at me, her tail wagging, but she cannot rise. In her eyes I can see her love for me and my heart breaks again. I move into the room and face them but only the dog notices. I back away silently towards the television.

Behind me is another door, a strong, large door that I somehow know leads outside. But can I leave? Walk out under the moonlight? While I think about what to do there comes three sharp knocks on the door. The watchers all look in sync at the door but none move nor answer.

And then I remember. It all floods back and overwhelms me. Everything. I turn to the door and open it inward. And she is there. An angel, blonde and radiant in the moonlight. My silvery moon mistress is here. I fall to my knees, sobbing before her. My hands lie in my lap, trembling. She looks sad and afraid to enter. We stare at each other, tears flowing.

I raise my right hand up to her. Hesitantly she steps forward and takes my hand. I expect us to miss, or pass through somehow, but the touch is solid. I expect her to flinch from the cold, frozen touch of the grave, but our flesh is warm and soft. My heart melts. I rise and she throws her arms around my neck, squeezing me with intensity as I wrap my arms around her lower back and lift her up to me. She cries with me. I have been dead for so long and now I feel so alive. I turn and lead, holding her hand as she follows me back to my room. The three watchers all ignore me but their eyes follow her. The old man smirks in disgust as we pass by. Maybe she should not be cavorting with the likes of me. Maybe she should not be here, wasting her time. I briefly see the eyes of the little boy but he is lost to me. The dog whimpers softly but her tail still wags in happiness.

Down the darkening hall she follows me. I close the door behind us. We are both barefoot. Shedding clothes in the dim shaft of moonlight I soon sit cross-legged in the center of the bed. She joins me, sitting on my lap, her legs wrapped around me. My arms encircle her lower back as she hugs me, resting her cheek against my forehead. We embrace in silence, revelling in the fire of our touches. My heart beats. I can feel the throb of my pulse again in the moonlight. Then she speaks. "I'm so sorry."

I hush her. I breathe deeply, unashamed to be alive again after so long in the grave. My fingertips slide up her back and tickle across her pale skin. She shivers at my touch. I can feel her muscles under her warm skin, and feel the ridge of her spine. My large, powerful hands have missed her. She caresses my back too, the way I love. All the miseries and pains of the world are gone.

"I love you," I whisper.

"I know," she answers.

Time passes so slowly. I find myself crying again and she holds me tight, trying to console and soothe me. She kisses my forehead and whispers, "I love you, Mr. Sad Eyes." My heart aches with those words.

"I know." Beloved. My love for her is incredible. I cannot control it. I wish I could; there would have been far less pain. I have loved once before, but she was a shadow, a lie, tricksy, false.

My love frightens me. Death is supposed to end the pain, but it cannot always do so. Death cannot stop love. It can only delay it. The more you open yourself to love, the more pain you must be willing to accept. The greatest betrayals come from those you trust the most.

"We cannot do this forever," she say meekly.

"My whole existence revolves around you. Not even death can stop my love. Our love." I know I would do anything for her, suffer anything. I would kill for her, neglect myself, use every ounce of energy and every fibre of my strength to protect her, to keep her safe. I have hurt others in the past, though I did not want to. I left a young man dying and alone, on the ruins of Castle Rock, under the Hunter's moon. He begged me to carry him there and leave him and I could not deny him. I have finished others, slain monsters. But some monsters are too strong for even the most powerful warrior.

She pulls apart from me. She lies naked, pale and beautiful, down on the bed, a pillow beneath her head. I lie between her legs as she wraps them around my back. I rest the side of my head upon her chest. She can feel me hot and strong, my chest between her legs. My elbows hug against her hips as she places her hands on my head, rubbing, petting, caressing my skin.

We soothe one another. Time passes. My heart aches again, but I care not. My voice is weak, but I whisper, "...I...am so sorry...for the pain I have caused you."

She holds me tighter. "We have hurt each other. I am sorry too. I love you." She kisses my head again. "You're my Davey."

I am such a weakling. Tears flow from me again, and I convulse silently in happiness. I have known so little happiness in my life. But all is fixed in the world right now.

"I wish this would last forever."

She caresses me. "Nothing lasts forever, baby."

My old nerve returns. "Doesn't it?" I reflect. My mind begins to grow cloudy again, thoughtful. Then I remember that she is not allowed to be here. We are forbidden. She will get in trouble. Someone does not want her to see me.

Who is it? A brother? I can't remember now. Death? Death and I are old friends. We have taught each other much. He came for me many times but I always defied him. He always failed to catch me. Or did he? The fog of confusion is back.

I am hurt again. I move, rising from the bed, pulling her with me. This time I lay on my back, pulling my muse down beside me. She lies against me now, my arm under her head, her leg draped across my bare hips, one arm over my chest, tickling my shoulder with her fingers, then my neck, then my chest. The world grows calm again. I can feel the whole universe revolving around us.

Another hour passes. The sun will return again. Time grows short. "I love you, baby."

"I know."

She kisses my chest. "What are we going to do?" she asks me.

My arm is under her head. I rub her arm. She caresses my chest and my other hand rubs her hand. "That has always rested with you. It has forever been your choice, your wants, your needs. You know how I feel. I want you to be happy forever, no matter what. I have tasted immortality. What use to be mortal again?" I kiss her.

"We can be together if you want. Forever if you wish. I will wait as long as I have to, as long as you want me to. I will do anything for you."

She starts to cry once more. Reaching up with her mouth, her lips kiss mine. I feel so much passion, anger, pain, love. I don't want it to stop.

She hugs me tight. "I'm so sorry..." her voice fails.

My fingers run through her silver, wavy hair. "I know. Every scar makes us stronger. But too many scars can burst us. I am not lost yet. I guess. I think I needed to be stabbed in the heart a few times to let out all the poison. You have made me a better man."

The end of our time is closing. Already the sun is closing in on us. My whole world changes with the coming of Dawn.

"I love you, princess."

She hugs me one last time. "I love you, Davey."

And then she is gone. Again. I know the ghosts in the front room are gone as well. Only the muffled sounds from the television seeping in to break the silence of my self-imposed tomb. I close my eyes again when the sunlight comes. I am already forgetting that she may be back again tonight. I sleep yet again. One more day. Motionless and dreamless I rest, dying further in my bed. Someday it will be time for me. Maybe tonight, if I am unlucky. Or lucky.

amity

by Jordan Elizabeth Mierek

A distinctive smell lingered on the wind: one of flowers, grass, and - dare I say it - death. The pebbles of the pathway through the cemetery were huge and rough, digging through the soles of my sneakers that I hadn't realized were so thin. Weeds fought for life, poking up through dirt dried by an arid summer. Vines crawled up the chain link fence, never happy with where they were, but always reaching for another place to call home. A deer grazed across the road, peering through the fence before dipping her head to the corn in the field for breakfast.

I passed from the newer graves with the planted pansies and decorations, into the world of ancients. Some of these gravestones had fallen over, toppled onto their sides by forces of nature or vandalism. No one planted flowers here; no plastic plaques sported grinning photographs. There were a couple flags for those who'd fought in wars: those reminders were few and far between.

The weathered graves crumbled. Some were shaped like logs, others like open books. One pillar pointed to the sky. Moss and ants crept across the stones, filling in the engraved words to make them unreadable.

I'd come to the end of the rural graveyard, turning on my heels beneath the metal archway proclaiming the area's name: Huxley Hill Cemetery.

I wandered back through the cemetery the way I'd come. It was tiny, as cemeteries went, since it only had one path. Still, it had the same aura that always drew me to cemeteries, that eerie the chance to be alone…yet surrounded.

I stumbled over one gravestone, nearly hidden in the weeds, and stopped to stare. The descendants had either moved away or forgotten; there were no flowers. How sad, to think that someday those who grew from your body would never bother to remember you.

I stuck my hands through the belt loops of my jeans, leaning back on one leg while reading the words practically lost now.

Amity Lansky, born 1891 and died in 1920.

She would have been twenty-nine when she passed away. That was all it said about her, no sentence about being a beloved daughter or devoted mother, no engraved weeping willow or cryptic paragraph, as some of the graves sported.

I crouched, tracing the 'A' of her first name. '*Amity*' It sounded lovely.

"You know her story, don't you?"

I jumped, a startled scream erupting from my mouth. The woman grinned at me, cocking her head to the side a bit. Her hair was pulled back into a bun, yet a few wayward strands fell over her face.

She laughed at my discomfort, her face crinkling pleasantly. She quirked her eyebrow in a way I'd always wished I could. "Weren't you expecting a ghost?"

I shook my head. Of course not. No one expected to see a ghost, not even in a cemetery. In any case, she wasn't what I imagined a ghost would look like. No pale floating sheets, no eerie black hole for a mouth. Her skin was pale, but not translucent. She certainly wasn't glowing. Her eyes were green, not hollow and haunted. Although she wore a long skirt and a blouse with a cameo at the collar, she looked vintage rather than historical. The skirt looked downright boho.

She laughed, reaching out to tap my arm. Creepy, yes, but not ghostly, and I didn't pull away. "I like coming to cemeteries just to think. So, do you know Amity's story?" She said the name gently, with a sweet, faraway look in her eyes. She wasn't wearing any make-up, yet her cheeks looked flushed.

"No. I just got here yesterday. My aunt is in the hospital from her gall bladder, so I'm watching my cousin. Well, he's seventeen, so I don't really have to 'watch' him, but he's still in high school, so my aunt thought it'd be best if someone was here to look after things." I pointed down the road, knowing I rambled. "They live in the white house down there a ways. Not too far. Walking distance."

The woman tapped her cameo. She was older than me, twenty-nine, maybe thirty, if I had to guess. "They just moved there?"

"Not really. My aunt moved there when she got married, so that's like…I dunno, maybe eighteen years ago."

"Ah." She moved to my side to stare at Amity. The sunlight made her brown hair glisten with streaks of gold. "Amity Lansky got married on her twenty-first birthday."

"Really?"

She nodded slowly. "The next year she had a daughter, but she gave the girl to her parents to raise."

"Do you know why?"

"Of course." The woman winked at me. "Her husband worked and her parents were elderly. Amity was their youngest. They moved in with them, you see. Amity was a poet. She was always writing, so she'd lock herself in her bedroom while they looked after the little girl. They tended the house. Took care of the garden."

"Sounds like a big help."

She chuckled dryly. "Then her husband died. They were terribly in love. He was everything to Amity. She was devastated, you see. She locked herself away. Her poems became dark and morbid."

"She didn't remarry?"

The woman sighed, closing her eyes. "Never. Her husband had a close friend who came after her hand, but she refused him. His name was Robert Andrews." She opened her eyes, peering at me as though the name meant something. When I didn't respond, she sighed again, even deeper now. "His descendants still run most of the town."

I didn't live here. How would I know?

"Amity died young," she continued, nodding at the grave. "There was a fever. It came on suddenly and took her away. Her little girl grew up, looked after her grandparents, married, and even raised her own children in the same house. Amity's descendants just moved, in fact. I believe your uncle bought it from them."

"That's…that's really cool." Coincidental, but cool. "I can't ask my uncle, though. He and my aunt got divorced a couple years ago. He moved to North Carolina."

"I know"," she whispered, her eyes suddenly wide. "Do you know what's truly sad about poor Amity Lansky?"

"I have no idea." The way she stared at me bordered on psychotic. It dawned on me I was alone in a cemetery in the middle of nowhere with a crazy woman, and no one knew where I'd gone. Even my cousin didn't know. Would he wonder when I wasn't home when he got off the bus?

"They say she killed her husband."

Whoa. Now that I really hadn't planned on. I backed away. I'd had enough of this story.

The woman grabbed my arms, staring at me with gigantic eyes. "Everyone said she did. He fell down the stairs, but they said she pushed him. They'd been the only ones home. She died with everyone thinking that. Even her daughter…"

"Let go of me!"

Her eyes softened and became misty. "She never got her poems published, either. Will you do me a favor, sweetie?"

"Yes!" Anything to get away from you.

Her hands slid off my arms and she stepped back. "My family has lived here a long time. Before Amity died, she said she'd written her poems in a diary. Could you find it, pet? I'm sure its still there." She smiled broadly. "That's a dear. Find it and bring it to me. It's in the attic, third floorboard from the window. There's only one window in the attic still, isn't there?"

"I guess so. I haven't been in the attic."

"Please look, won't you? I'll still be here when you come back. I'm always here."

She really did look like the type who spent all her time wandering cemeteries. If she wondered why I ran from her without saying goodbye, she certainly didn't call after me. Truth be told, I thought her loony. Surely there was a desperate madness in her eyes. Besides, hiding stuff in floorboards only works in movies and books.

Still, I'm not one to lack the curiosity gene. I let myself into my aunt's house, locking the door behind me in case the woman from the cemetery followed. I took the stairs two at a time, finding the door to the attic unlocked.

Cobwebs littered the corners of the stairs, yet they didn't creak and the electric light worked. There was indeed only one window. Sunlight poured in, although the glass panes were filthy. I counted three floorboards from the window and kicked it. Nothing.

There were boxes everywhere and an old couch, proving my aunt still used the space. I ran back downstairs and to the garage, stealing a minute to glance out the front door for signs of the woman.

I took a screwdriver back to the attic. As I jammed the tip into the dirt around the floorboard, I considered how insane this was. A crazed woman from a country cemetery tells me to pry up a floorboard in my aunt's attic looking for a diary from 1920, so I do it. At least my aunt would understand. She'd probably laugh about it, so long as the floorboard went back down. Maybe I should have brought a hammer.

I wondered if the woman had told my aunt to look for the diary. Maybe she told everyone in the whole town there was a diary hidden in their floorboards...yet she had known about the single window.

Lucky guess? She might've studied the house from outdoors.

An audible snap made my stomach sink, but in the next second, a corner of the floorboard poked up. I forced it the rest of the way with the screwdriver's handle, watching dirt rain into the hole. A piece of red fabric peaked out from inside.

It ripped at the mercy of my fingers. Underneath lay a leather-bound diary. My breath caught in my throat. For a second, I stared at it, and then I opened the cover slowly, knowing it for the precious thing it was.

I carefully turned each page. The woman hadn't lied after all. Most of the brittle, ancient pages had poems - good poems, too. Very insightful and enlightening, and dare I even say it, I liked them better than Emily Dickinson's. Hers are good, but confusing, while these were clear, to the point, and romantic. Not so much in the love sense, although some were, but all were artfully written. They spoke to me in a way most poetry didn't. Some pages told about Amity's day.

"*I walked to the cemetery to put a rose on Uncle's grave*" and
"*I wrote a letter to Cousin today*" were two that stood out to
me.

I could envision this in print at bookstores.

Suddenly the date on one page caught my eye. I stared at it in
dawning horror. Flipping ahead, the poems became dark and truly
Gothic with raw anger and hatred, terror and devastation that made
them exquisitely delicious. I flipped back to the horrifying day
note she had entered, the handwriting visibly shaking. This was
what was going to make the book a bestseller.

"*Robert Andrews came over. He tried to kiss me. Sylvester was
enraged. He ordered Robert out. They fought. I tried to stop them,
but Robert pushed Syl down the stairs. He's dead, my Syl. He died.
I sat beside him and wept, but Robert laughed. He has said that if
I tell anyone how Syl died, he'll kill my baby. I won't let Robert kill
my baby. No one would believe me if I said. Robert's father is the
mayor. No one will believe me. I won't say. They don't know Robert
came over. They'll think I did it. They can't condemn me. No one
can prove it. I am female.*"

I read it over again, the ink faded and blurry, yet still there,
still real. Once it was published, everyone would know Robert had
done the deed. Amity's name would be cleared. Sylvester Lanksy's
murder would be proven. Thrill bubbled in my veins as I clutched
the diary, mindful of its fragility, and ran back to the cemetery.

The woman wasn't there. I found Amity's grave, and held the
diary out to the fading letters. "Look, Amity! I found it. I know
you were innocent." Foolish to talk to the dead perhaps, but I was
too excited to keep quiet.

"I knew you'd find it!

She scared me again, that woman.

"You were right. How did you know?"

She lightly touched the diary. "You'll work to get it published?"

"Of course. These poems are great. Um, where's her husband's grave?"

"Yonder." She pointed across the path. "His parents were still alive when he died. When Amity died, they didn't want his grave near his murderer's."

"But she didn't kill him. Robert Andrews did."

"I know." She smiled sadly. "Now everyone will know."

"How did you know?" Something slipped out of the diary's back. "Hey, what's this?" I bent to pick it up a photograph, brittle and torn, so old it was hard to see.

I turned it over, reading where someone had written Amity on the back. I flipped it back to see the front, squinting at the picture. Amity had dark hair pulled back in a bun. She wore a dress with a cameo fastened to the high collar.

"No way." I raised my eyes to the woman, but I was alone in the cemetery save for the dead underfoot.

For a second, the strong odor of violets overpowered me and an insane, intoxicating giggle floated in the wind, but the next second, all I heard was the creak of the cemetery's single oak, and all I smelled was grass.

who's afraid of the dark?

by Terri Evert Karsten

I have always liked the dark, that cozy blanket of shadow wrapping me in its warmth and hiding me from garish lights and strangers. The darkness deadens ordinary sounds, and the murmuring leaves whisper promises. Doors to other worlds open wider in a starless night, mysterious and inviting. Yes, I had always liked walking in the dark, until that night.

A concert at the Church of Saint-Sulpice in Paris had kept us out late, and the Luxembourg Garden had closed at sunset. We would have to walk the long way around, but none of us minded. Summer warmth lingered into the night as the four of us waved goodbye to our friends.

Chattering, we left the church behind and rounded the first corner. A sudden breeze rattled the leaves overhead. My skin prickled with goosebumps.

"I thought this was summer." Suzanne wrapped her sweater closer.

Jeanette and Marie laughed, teasing our Southern friend about the coming winter.

I would have joined their laughter, but something in the dark reached out. An almost overpowering sense of evil brushed past, and I stopped abruptly.

"What is it?" Jeannette turned her teasing to me. "Did you see a ghost?"

"Something is following us." I don't know why I said 'something' instead of 'someone' but that was right. Something was out there, and it had seen us. The street lamps cast a feeble light, forming grotesque shadows of fenced-in trees and empty parked cars. There was no wind, nothing to break the heavy, deadening stillness.

"Don't be silly," Jeannette said, laughing. The sound echoed along the concrete and asphalt, but when its rumors faded, silence, palpable in its intensity, surrounded us.

Jeannette turned abruptly and walked on. "There's nothing there," she insisted.

We turned the next corner. This was the last, longest side of the garden, a narrow street crowded with small dingy houses facing the garden park. Not a single window in the whole row was lit. A car sped past, the headlights' harsh glare leaving me blinded and exposed, and then the street was empty once more. Ancient street lamps flickered through the leaves of the trees.

As we passed, one of the lights flared and then sputtered out, and something creaked open.

We weren't alone.

A malevolence crept behind us, growing stronger with each step we took along this dark stretch. I was afraid to turn and look.

To my right a tall iron fence separated the garden from the sidewalk. Thick bushes stretched through the railing, trying to escape their enclosure.

At a crack in the pavement, I stumbled brushing against the sharp branches, and jerked back in alarm.

"What is it?" Marie clutched my arm. "A thorn?"

I shook my head, but didn't answer, unwilling to admit I thought I felt a dozen tiny hands pinching me. Overhead, something laughed with cruel amusement.

Each step became harder than the last. My feet felt glued to the pavement and lifting them, one after the other, became a battle of wills, my own dogged deternmination to reach home and safety, against the evil will intent on destroying us totally. Marie, Suzanne and I linked arms, and pushed forward.

Jeannette pulled away, scoffing. "Silly nightmares." Her hips swished disdainfully. "Just scaring yourselves, like babies." She walked ahead, defying the fear.

We reached the midpoint of the long sidewalk, with the empty street stretching out before us and behind us. It was the darkest point, the point furthest from either end, furthest from the world we knew, the safe and ordinary world. Jeannette, ten or twelve steps ahead of us now, was nearly invisible in the thick darkness. I was just about to call out to her, to warn her not to go too far ahead, when the suffocating force hit us, a swirling maelstrom of dark, all claws and teeth and shrieking pain.

Like a cold wave from the sea, the pure malice and corruption of the being swept over us, and I clung desperately to my friends. I screamed, the sound distant as if it came from somewhere far beyond me. Another raw scream, closer this time, tore at my ears, a hideous wail of terror and despair. It was followed by a mocking laugh, a laugh so evil that I still shiver to think of it.

I hung on, fighting the mind-numbing malevolence. Dizzy, confused by the swirling darkness, I felt blind and alone, but I hung on.

Then as suddenly as it had hit, the wave passed us, and we fell to our knees, choking back sobs. Ahead of us, the feeble light of the next street lamp flickered back on. Without a word, we rose and ran toward that light.

We reached the end of the street and hurried on, never daring to look back, Rounding the corner, we burst into the next street. A door clicked softly shut behind us.

"Where is Jeannette?" Marie asked.

None of us answered, afraid that speaking would make the horror true. We had all heard the laugh; the triumphant laugh of a torturer whose victim has given in.

"She was ahead of us," Suzanne said finally. "She's probably already home. Maybe she made it through before IT hit."

None of us believed that, but it gave us an excuse to go on instead of turning back.

We arrived home without further words. Jeannette wasn't there of course. We all knew she wouldn't be, but we pretended she would come back in her own time and let the fiction save us the admission of cowardice.

The next morning Jeannette was still missing and an article

on the front page of the morning paper reported an unidentifiable body found next to the garden where we had been walking the night before. Official cause of death was listed as a hit and run accident. We never told them otherwise.

And I don't walk in the dark anymore.

REVENANT

by Sean Krage

I'm not done yet, boy . . .

The voice was gnarled, low and stinging. It awoke Timothy from a sleep he could not remember. He now stood motionless inside a dome of vines, their branches entwined like a cage. Above him the red light of a setting sun scattered through the leafy web. At his feet, swirling about the dirt, were the leaves of yesterday. Two gloves he might have been wearing lay inside the chaos. As he looked around, unnerved by it all, his pocket began to vibrate and the chimes of an old TV show rang softly in the enclosure. What that song was, or who was calling him were mysteries to Timothy, but these queries did not compare to the most abrasive question. He had awoken standing, trapped in disbelief, pressing a bitterly cold knife to his wrist, not hard enough to bleed him, just hard enough to show intent. In that cage, he stood alone, swelling with the fear of losing everything he failed to recall.

Timothy slowly opened his fingers and released the knife. His right hand cautiously entered the writhing pocket, feeling the phone for clues. Behind him, a rustle of leaves stirred his hopes and he cocked his head hard. Standing in the tall, ornamental oval opening of the dome was a young man with lazy eyes and disheveled brown hair. The man raised his chin high as he took in the vines above. A goofy grin linked his cheeks once he stepped inside the beautiful artistry, strolling without care. Sticking his thumbs between the straps of his brown pack and shoulders, he took a wide stance.

"Wow, pretty cool."

The voice rang in mystery. Timothy wanted desperately for the man to tell him everything.

"Looks important, doesn't it?" As he swung his eyes about the dome, nodding in meaningless acknowledgement, the man saw the blade at Timothy's feet. "What the hell, Dude? You gonna cut down the vines or something?" The admiration fled his voice; his smile fleeted. "That yours?"

Timothy slowly shook his head, hoping to drag slow the world around him. The man continued on, changing the subject.

"You gonna answer your phone, Dude? Alex is probably looking for you after what you said to her."

Timothy took the cell and thumbed it open, every cautious movement drawing attention to itself. He put it to his ear and did not dare to speak, hoping this Alex would reveal all. With a loud burst, the woman shook Timothy.

"Hey . . ." A long sigh followed that filled the dome with possibility. "Are Holly and Sam with you?"

Nothing about the voice was familiar and Timothy's mind burned with frustration. He brought the back of his hand to his forehead, breathing heavily through his mouth.

"Yeah, I, um." He rubbed his brow with fervor. "Yeah I think Sam is here?"

"And Holly's on her way."

A swelling began to build behind Timothy's eyes and at the back of his throat that told of screams within. It was silenced by Sam dropping his backpack and speaking obnoxiously loud.

"Is that Alex? Hey Alex! We're with Timothy. So I think, you know, head out, or whatever." From his pack he pulled a slip of paper.

The voice on the other side continued. "Tell Sam we're not leaving yet." Timothy saw a map unfold in Sam's hands. "Tim . . . Listen . . ." Another sigh stole the peace. There came a pause, timed by a racing heartbeat.

Timothy wanted an explanation. He wanted something, something big. No words, no matter how diabolic, could worsen his world.

"I'm sorry, Tim, but you obviously don't think I'm serious about those seeds. You think the Almyt are a joke, and I get that. I understand."

A shaking heat now filled his skull. Timothy wanted to scream, knowing it would get him an answer or two, but an indescribable desire and fear to be exactly who these two wanted him to be kept his composure. He had to let something out.

"What . . ." The words sat at the edge of his lips afraid to touch the phone.

Sam stood, brow furrowed and biting his lower lip.

"Just apologize, Dude. She knows you didn't mean it."

More words without meaning. In his anger, Tim found a bit of humor that he could guess as to who they were, but had no stories to give confidence. As he considered the ease of giving up and screaming, there was a slow descent of memories. He closed his eyes, and waited as Alex continued.

"Well, anyways, Mr. McNally finally called; says we can head over to the house." Her voice softened and loudened without rhythm, as if she looked around. "So tell that to Sam. And he knows we're not going till I can see the house. I mean there's no reason to be here if we don't, and did you guys find the well? Sam said he thought you found the well."

The word 'well' broke every chain around Timothy. The retreating tension let loose a flood of overwhelming joy. He remembered looking for a well, and in that well was Almyt, a bright red seed with ungodly importance. Alex's world revolved around these seeds, and had for months. Alex, who was his girlfriend, his fiancée, his reason, wanted nothing more than Almyt, and her wants were his. Of these waves of thoughts, one struck him hardest. In his pocket, where his phone had danced, rested an Almyt. It was heavy, translucent, and as bulky as a stone.

Timothy shot his free hand across his body and gripped the hidden treasure. Neither Sam nor Alex knew it was there. Its discovery was the last memory he had before a seizure of a million foreign memories beat him into unconsciousness: Stories he was never told, a daughter and wife he had never met. The seed had powers unimaginable with a weight that had squeezed his lungs and drenched his mind in obscure tales. It was as if an entire hall of men had spoken to him at once and then vanished when he awoke. But as he stood there, he knew at least one remained, roaming his desires, something 'other.'

Tim suddenly became aware of time and the look on his face. He attempted to cover.

"No, sorry, Babe. We didn't find the well. We're standing in a, something. An orchard I think, but, yeah, no well."

"Damn it. Damn it, all right. I was really hoping."

"I know you were, Alex, and I'm sorry. Sorry I didn't believe you." Tim picked up his gloves and put them on, though he was sweating with excitement. "It's getting cold out. I was just wanting to leave, you know? I'm not really angry."

He forced out a ridged laugh that stood alone. Alex ignored it.

"Yeah, I know it's fine. I'm in the field we walked through, off of the road, just outside the woods you're in. Come on out so we can reach McNally's before dark."

"Yeah, sure. See you in a bit." Timothy shut the phone and felt the Almyt, spinning it slowly in his pocket. He bit the side of his lip as a long dead feeling of control rose up. Timothy noticed Sam again. His friend attempted a guess.

"So . . . what's up? We doin' anything, or . . ."

Tim picked up the knife, swinging it with flicks of his wrist and walking around to jar what else he could, trying to remember what those thousand voices had said. There was another rustle outside the enclosure and a young woman with thick blonde hair matted with leaves began to take shape down the path.

"You guys back here?" She was bending and twisting past the invasive branches. "Sam? Tim?"

Sam's mouth cracked open as he took in Timothy's strange behavior. "Uh, yeah Holly, we're here."

She stepped into the dome, pulling the remains of nature from her pink sweatshirt. Her face was smooth and fitted with an inevitable smile.

"You guys find anything?"

Sam shrugged, arms close to his body. He widened his eyes and gave a goofy, closed mouth look at Tim, hoping to be buddies again, but Tim ignored him. He was thinking of the Almyt, the knife at his wrist, and a new name: Edgar.

"Let's go you guys; Alex is waiting for us in the field." He jumped past his two friends and bull-rushed through the branches that had troubled Holly. "We need to hurry." With his mind returning, he took off to find his Alex.

The excitement of memory sent Timothy bounding through the brush with energy that once filled his life. In his mind he scrambled to pick up the pieces some ghostly meteor had ravaged. He broke branch and barrier to recall himself, but some memories still roamed the fog. In front of it all stood the name Edgar, a long-dead man that had discovered the Almyt seeds in a mysterious well. It had been months since Alex first showed Tim the news articles of Edgar's arrest and disappearance, but they were now fresh in his mind. The famous story had spun a web of legends the four friends now waded through. As Tim charged through the underbrush, whispering the man's name, the wind came, quick and sudden. And then it spoke.

Let me save them . . .

Tim stopped and swung his head around. The wind died and he strained his eyes and ears, but found nothing. He then took off again, somehow resilient to the oddities he heard. As he ran, his mind formed an image of Edgar, one of a husband and a father. He saw the bearded farmer, shovel in hand, tall and gaunt. He saw him sitting at a damp, rotting desk, screaming at papers in a dirt-floor basement. But as he ran, Tim realized he was not imagining, but remembering. He was not frightened, however, for the Other within calmed his mind.

Tim burst forth from the wood's edge and halted; he now stared at the crossed arms and face of Alex. Behind her towered hills that tore the beauty of Earth; their cliffs and ledges were abundant with the grey of crumbling rock. Somehow, they appeared much older than the fields before them.

Somewhere around him the sun sat on the horizon. Alex approached with intensity, but she caved and hugged him tightly. Tim swelled again in frustration as an unknown past littered his thoughts. He wanted to scream and recalled all he could of the Almyt.

But as Alex spoke, his heart slowed. Her touch let him breathe easier, and the mysterious thoughts now fed his energy. He became excited to uncover what he could. He let Alex go and walked past her, hands out, as though trying to grab the untouched fields.

"Who was Edgar?" Tim could feel her eyes piercing him, as though she sensed the Almyt.

"I told you the story, but I know you don't care."

"I'm sorry, Alex. I know I was rude, but tell me again. I want to know."

With a tone that warned of anger, she spoke of the man consuming Tim's mind. "Edgar was the farmer who found the Almyt, those red seeds I'm looking for. Legend says if you place one on the place of someone's death, they are safe from Hell.

"And what happens if you plant the seeds?"

"Tim, it doesn't matter. Edgar was crazy. He killed his wife and daughter. It's just a legend."

Alex's words pulled more memories from the fog, but these were not Tim's. He described them as they appeared, speaking towards the hills.

"Edgar convinced the sheriff to take him back to his home, where he promised to show him their bodies."

"Tim . . ."

"The sheriff did and then returned . . . without Edgar."

"Tim, none of that matters. Edgar's been dead for fifty years. We're just looking for the Almyt and papers, if they even exist."

There came a noise, soft and loud. It was the wind, and then the sky. Tim looked to his right. In the distance, the tall grass sloped down and curved with the hills, turning into a ravine that consumed the East. Tim tried to understand the whisper as Alex continued.

"The only legend I care about is if the Almyt are truly from Iceland."

It's growing in the basement . . .

"I mean, it would be so cool if I could prove that ancient Vikings had reached Minnesota."

I must stop it . . .

She did not hear it. She could not hear the rising and falling breath growing from under the treeless roots and stones that littered the ravine. The noises were meant for Tim.

Breaking from the trees behind them were Holly and Sam, their laughs and giggles burying the dark howls of the wind. They ran into the field, joking in ways lost to their friends. Sam grabbed Holly from behind and hoisted her into the air.

"You're going to regret that!"

He carried her, squirming and screaming, to his friends and dropped her down beside them. She shoved him with play and pulled at the bottom of her shirt.

"What's up? What we doing?"

Timothy and Alex stood tense. Timothy studied the ravine as Alex explained.

"This might be our only chance at visiting Edgar's old house. The well was just a rumor, but the report said the sheriff left the Almyt and evidence against Edgar in the house."

Behind her words, came the wind once more. It rose as she spoke and took to life on the ridge of the hills. Tim's companions crossed their arms to battle the cold as Tim stood loose. He listened as the moans went from wailings to words. He then began to translate.

"There's a basement. She died in the basement."

Alex sighed, still raw from before. "Tim, shut up. Stop mocking me."

"It's all hidden in the basement. He left them in the basement."

Timothy saw Edgar, sweating and shaking, burying an Almyt into the cellar dirt.

"He tried to use the Almyt. He didn't know what he was doing."

Timothy now saw faces and a house he had never seen. He saw Edgar and his nameless, sullen wife, crying over a mound of rubble, screaming to the ends of the Earth. Onto the mound, Edgar placed another shining Almyt. This one he did not bury.

All thoughts were clear and unwelcome; Timothy wanted them gone, but someone wanted them there. He could not turn away. They were his now, and rested beside his own. As the new arrivals beckoned to him, Alex shook her head and motioned to Holly and Sam.

"Come on you two. Stay here if you want, Tim. I really don't care anymore."

The troupe hustled, armed with packs and flashlights, under the watch of crooked trees and a moon dancing between clouds. The sun had slipped behind ridged bluffs, abandoning the four to navigate the rocky dry ravine, guessing at every step. The distance between them grew and shrank as the terrain eased and threatened under a bright moonlight. Timothy tried to match Alex's pace with anxiety urging, but was left in her wake beside the chatty Sam and Holly. The neglect did not bother him; all he wanted was to talk, anything to keep the voice at bay.

"Why do you guys think the sheriff left Edgar in his home?"

The two cared little of what he said; they were just happy to be with their friends. They suffered through Tim's meaningless theories until the trio spotted Alex, waiting at the ravine's end. It rose up and into a clearing where the young woman stood tall and alone. Before her was their destination, and the sight of Edgar's dying home stirred the Other inside. Tim could feel it thicken, excited by what was to come.

The house they sought slouched in the foreground of a mountain displaced. From the rolling hills that dominated the area, a single column of stone rose up and shadowed the structure. The home resembled the backdrop of a high school play. The front was uncomfortably basic; there was a door in the center, flanked by windows, with a roof peaking just above it. Its yellow paint was multicolored from age, and cracks spider-webbed the right side. Fragments of roof and ceiling shot out of the top, revealing fallen debris. The left side had been taken out by a collection of trees that lay gathered in the destruction they created. The right side had been consumed by the mountain behind it. "Perhaps a mudslide," Timothy considered, pretending to feel like himself.

The four marched quietly forward, looking around, as though it were a trap. Holly was the first to step into the chaos.

"Was there a fire?"

There was no sign of fire damage, but that's all anyone could compare it to. Walls were half missing, the furniture was completely stained, and the floor bulged up, as though something was pushing. Fate had been cruel to this deeply wounded home.

Lying about the front door was the rubble of stairs that once led to the balcony before them. A few steps remained, clinging to the wall that split the house; the rest had been demolished by the crowns of the trees. To their left, and under the fallen giants, was a dining room littered with itself. From walls to dishes and chairs, nothing was spared. Beyond the branches and destruction was a raised kitchen. The trees had left the aged appliances untouched, but nature took no prisoners. The refrigerator door hung by a single hinge while the sink and cupboards had been jarred from their spots. Everything was stained by dirt and time; scratch marks seemed to count the years. Surveying all of this were two doors on the unreachable balcony above the kitchen.

To their right must have been a living room. A bearskin rug lay with a wide-eyed stare, screaming to be freed from the mountain of dirt that had engulfed the far half of the room. From outside Timothy had thought the house rested against the raging mound, but now could tell the beast had moved in. Out of the mess stuck a dissolving couch and fireplace. Holly screamed as rodents, thrilled by the newcomers, regrouped from the cushions to the wall. Sam pulled her back, but did no other consoling as he stood smiling, challenged by the wasted stairs.

"What do you suppose is up there? I bet I could climb this and see."

No one responded and Sam stepped eagerly forward onto a mound of rubble. As he readied himself, Holly called out.

"Sam . . ." The rest of her plea faded.

Sam leapt with a grunt and he landed belly-first, legs hanging, onto the shaking and creaking steps.

"Be careful, honey!"

Sam stretched out his arms and began to crawl, the wooden steps calling out with every motion. Holly gasped and protested as the other two looked around, Alex to the mound of dirt in the living room, Timothy at the floor below the steps. A light began to grow from beneath the floor boards and Timothy somehow knew only he could behold it.

Don't let him go upstairs . . .

"Did you see that?" Alex swung her light to the living room. Cautiously, she followed it. "I saw something flash, from the cave-in."

Shaking her head, Holly followed Alex.

"I can't watch this. Make sure he doesn't kill himself, Tim."

But Timothy could not hear her as the voice grew with the brightening, green light.

He can't go upstairs . . . I need more time! Send me back to Hell, now!

Timothy wobbled, breathing heavily as he uttered quiet non-sense. Sam had almost reached the top. From the living room, Alex shouted.

"Yes! Tim we found an Almyt!"

Then Holly screamed.

"Is that a body?!"

Don't let him go upstairs!

Timothy charged the hanging steps Sam crawled. Like a mad man he slammed his fists and forearms onto the bottom of the remaining stairs. It gave way instantly, taking with it Sam and half the rotted balcony. The bulging, warped floor below collapsed from their landing and everything disappeared in a torrent of crashes. Timothy fell back into the entryway as wood and dust took to the air. The entire dining room caved loudly into the basement. The emerald light from below filled the house and Timothy could do nothing but look away.

"TIM? SAM! WHAT HAPPENED!?

Holly and Alex rushed back, their flashlights swinging in all directions. They flanked Timothy and stopped, both of their lights fixed on the destruction. The two lifted him to his feet, though he could not bear the light.

"Are you okay, Tim?!"

Timothy pointed forward as the dust settled. Holly ran to the edge and the other two followed behind. The girls' lights settled on the legs of Sam, whose body lay buried under debris in the basement.

"Sam! Sam are you okay?!"

"Tim, what happened?"

The three prayed and watched as Sam slowly rolled over and pushed aside the loose wood that lay on him. With eyes closed and coughing from his bloody mouth, he extended a hand and gave a smiling thumbs up. "What the hell just happened?"

Alex began to move her flashlight around in the mess as Holly swung hers, looking for a way down.

Sam sat up and shrugged, dusting himself off and looking over the rubble he sat in. "Holy shit, is that a tree?"

As Timothy grew tolerant of the light, he finally saw where his friend had fallen. In the far right corner of the basement was the damp, rotting desk he had seen Edgar frantically work. The papers were still there, stacked and scattered, somehow spared from the collapse. But what drew his attention was the source of the light meant only for him. On the left wall of the basement was a tree, thick and twisted. A crystal blue bark wrapped the trunk and a dozen branches, pulsing with an echoing moan. The sapphire fiend was rooted in the dirt and concrete wall and gave off a warm green light that struck the being inside Tim.

It's going to bloom . . . Send me back to Hell you stupid boy!

From the branches hung a mixture of what was once the basement stairs, torn apart by the thing as it grew, and the remains of some poor soul. Ribs, femurs, and others stuck out from the thick trunk and ends of branches. The beast covered the entire Western wall.

If that tree blooms I will never live again . . . I need more time!

As Holly scolded Sam, Alex walked around the pit to the Western edge. Timothy remained still, burdened by the Other inside. He stared comatose, unseen in the darkness his companions suffered, as his girlfriend stepped onto a branch and quickly scaled the short, thick beast of nature. Holly shrieked with protest, but soon quieted as Alex took control from the basement floor.

"Can you walk, Sam?"

"I should be all right."

Alex helped Sam to his feet as he triumphantly raised his hands.

"Did you see that Tim? That must have scared the hell out of you!"

Alex approached the rotting desk, scanning with her flashlight. She began to leaf through the papers as Sam and Holly threw out questions about the tree and the Almyt Alex had found. But Tim did not rejoice in their discoveries. He heard very little of what they said for he was now a prisoner to the voice and soul roaming inside.

Listen to me . . . My wife hung herself at the top of the steps.

From the mess, Alex drew a slip of paper.

The rope still hangs there . . .

She eyed the document for a second and grinned wide.

"Wow, listen to this you guys. Edgar must have been one messed up dude."

Tim walked slowly to the ledge above the tree as Alex read the document aloud.

"I can now say with the highest of certainty that these Almyt seeds are the cause of my curse. My daughter's death was no accident, but punishment for taking these rituals and seeds from the well. She died in the avalanche weeks ago and now my wife has taken her life as well."

"So that body we found was his daughter's?" asked Holly.

Tim dropped to his knees and felt the edge of basement ceiling, feeling for what the Other wanted. He found the hanging noose, and pulled it into the light. He stuck his hand into his pocket and grabbed the Almyt as Alex continued.

"Everything is falling apart. That stupid sheriff disturbed the Almyt protecting my daughter. And now I am about to pay for planting one . . ."

I need to go back. I need to save what the sheriff ruined, boy!

". . . where my wife hung herself. If that tree blooms, her soul will be traded for mine. I will not have this. I will save us all."

Tim placed the Almyt at the edge of the crater and stood once more, holding the slipknot in eminence. He could no longer hear his Alex and closed his eyes.

I wasn't done when you lifted my Almyt seed, boy . . .

"To those who read this, I, Edgar Brown, have left this world. I have found a ritual to save my loved ones from Hell . . ."

Alex quieted, and began reading to herself.

You're going to pay for touching that Almyt . . .

Alex's eyes glazed over and she pulled the Almyt she had found from her pack. "Wow, this guy actually believed these protected the dead. He claims he used another one and offed himself."

Sam chuckled and Holly sighed.

"Okay Alex, can we go now? You found what we came for."

Alex nodded and began gathering the paper. Sam went to help her, but noticed Timothy.

"Tim, what are you doing?"

Timothy calmly placed the noose around his neck and pulled it tight, eyes closed.

I was not through, boy . . .

The women shined their lights on their lone friend.

"Tim?"

Timothy opened his eyes, the red flare of Edgar's past shining through. His companions shouted his name again, but he did not respond. Holly ran to him, but it was no use. Nothing of this world was going to stop Edgar. The shell of what was once Timothy smiled, and breathed in deep.

" . . . Goodbye . . ."

And with a leap, Edgar returned once more to the search of his loved ones.

simon and the ghost

by Jeremy Mortis

It was around eight o'clock and I was working on a calculus problem in the library. Eddie was waiting for me to finish so we could start our quest into the mad scientist's lab in *Monsters and Mayhem* when I felt a cold breeze brush the back of my neck. A quick glance to my right showed me that the window was shut tight. My first thought was that the air conditioner was on.

"Help me." A voice whispered.

I glanced around, looking to see if someone else was having homework problems like me but no such luck. All the desks around me were as empty as a bunch of beer cans on Sunday morning.

"Help me. You're the only one who can." The whisper was more urgent than last time.

The voice was coming from my right. I got up and walked around the stacks. What I saw almost stopped my heart. It was a white form similar to thick smoke or fog.

"Ok, I'm dreaming. Hopefully this isn't the one where I'm standing in front of my English class wearing a cheerleader uniform." Maybe I should have gotten more than a couple of hours sleep in the last week or two.

"You're not dreaming. I need your help. You're the only one I've found who can see and hear me."

My knees went weak so I grabbed the dark wooden table to hold myself up. Once I was steady, I yanked my backpack off the table and then hot-stepped it to the exit. I was at the library door when the voice said, "Stop! Someone is going to die tonight and you are the only one who can stop it from happening."

"Yeah, that's great, Casper, but you're not real. Now I'm going to my room to get some sleep." The librarian looked at me and shushed as I threw the door open.

The night air was surprisingly warmer then the library. There were a few people out walking, smoking cigarettes and talking. Ah, a sense of normal, every day college life; could anything be better?

"I'm still here," the voice whispered in my ear.

"Please go away. I'm not the guy you're looking for," I pleaded.

The figure was growing more solid, so I could make out some details. By the curves of her body I could tell it was woman. She was wearing a hood that hid everything but her mouth.

"I don't get to chose. You heard my voice therefore you are the one I am looking for," she said with a voice so commanding it could make the sun rise at midnight.

"But I'm no hero. I'm a just a guy who likes playing video games and watching sci-fi movies." And talks with imaginary ghosts, I might have added, but didn't.

"That doesn't matter. Either you play hero or you get a new best friend, me, for the rest of you life."

The first thought that popped into my head was, could she do that? Then I started to worry that if she did, what would I do? Having a permanent air conditioner hovering nearby was no way to live.

I hurried toward the dorms. Even with the poorly lit walkways I knew I was heading the right direction. The sound of music blaring was my own version of a lighthouse.

I was half way to my dorm room when I heard her say, "I'm still here. You are wasting valuable time."

Ok, walking away didn't work. Maybe I should call a priest. But what were the chances that I could find one that would be willing to make a house call? That and the last time I went into a church, the roof starting leaking on my head. If that's not a sign to stay out, I don't know what is.

"Look, all I want you to do is go talk to her. Prevent her killer from getting to her. Nothing dangerous or life threatening, just go talk to her."

"That's all?" I was more than skeptical.

"Yes. Then I will go away and never bother you again."

Could it really be that easy? Just go talk to some random person? Somehow I didn't think so, but it beat the hell out of living in a walk-in freezer.

"Ok, hit me with the details."

"Her name is Melissa. She is about my height with blond hair. She will be wearing a pink hoodie. In about two minutes she will be walking from the parking lot to her dorm room."

"Which dorm is hers?"

"Macgregor."

I ran across campus hoping to make it in time. The wind whipped my face with a thousand tiny barbs as the deep freeze kept pace with me. My legs burned by the time I reached the residence hall. I took a quick look around as I forced air into my lungs.

"Where is she? I'm too late, aren't I?"

"No. She's on her way. Just be patient."

I was about to yell at my ectoplasmic tormentor when a blond appeared next to a blue four door. As she turned toward me I muttered "Jackpot." She was wearing a pink sweatshirt and looking for something in her purse.

Ok, I found her. Now what do I do? I mean I've never been good at starting conversations with strangers. My roommate Eddie was the one who got the proverbial ball rolling in our friendship. I'll just yell her name and then ask for her notes for some class. Hopefully that will work.

"Hey, Melissa."

I heard the words, but it wasn't my voice. Melissa turned to her right and smiled.

"Hey, Chad, I thought you were going to the Theta Pi party tonight."

"I am. I just wanted to stop by and see if you wanted to come with."

"Sure just let me drop off my books," she said and then ran past me like I was invisible.

I let out a sigh of relief. I was done. The girl was saved and I didn't get punched in the face. Now I was free to go play *Steamed Aged Sorcery* guilt free.

"What the hell are you doing?"

The ice age was back and it showed no signs of stopping.

"What? You said to make sure Melissa was safe. She's with Chad. No one is going to mess with her. Did you see him? He's built like a linebacker."

"You know for someone so smart you have a difficult time following directions."

"What are you talking about? I did exactly what you asked. So, why aren't you going off to heaven or wherever you go when you're done?"

"My business isn't finished. I said to go talk to her and prevent her killer from getting to her."

"Well Chad is going to do that. Isn't he?" I asked.

"No. He isn't," she said with a tone that reminded me of one my teachers. They would stop and wait for the answer to come to me. Seconds felt like hours and sweat slowly rolled down my back. Finally, Eureka! I figured it out, and once again my stomach hit the floor.

"He's the killer isn't he?"

"Not yet, but soon. It's up to you."

"I'm not getting in the car. You're drunk." I heard Melissa yell, as I felt a surge of strength in my legs.

"I'm not drunk. I just had a few, that's all. Now get your ass in the car," Chad yelled back.

"I don't care. I'll call you tomorrow, after you've slept it off." Melissa said as she slammed the car door.

Chad ran to her side and grabbed her. "Get in the freaking car right now, or I'm going to put you in the car."

I ran and grabbed Chad by the shoulder and said, "Chad, seriously, just let her go and call it a night."

"Get the hell out of here, jackass. This isn't your problem." He said as he shoved me into a parked car. I lost my balance and went down on my ass. Which I must admit hurt, but not as much as it hurt my pride.

"You have to stop him. You can do this, Simon. I believe in you," the ghost whispered in my ear.

I jumped and grabbed Chad by the shoulder again. As he turned to say something I punched him square in the nose. Blood exploded all over Chad's face as he went straight down to the pavement. My fist stung like a hundred angry bees had just paid it a visit.

I felt a warm breeze brush by my cheek as a voice whispered in my ear, "Thank you, Simon." I turned to look and I saw her misty form disappearing like fog in the rising sun. As she as disappeared she pulled her hood away from her face and I saw Melissa's face staring back at me.

yankee inn

by Jordan Elizabeth Mierek

I flipped the sign hanging on the front door to "open" and faced my staff. Three waitresses stood near the fireplace, laughing over something. Mary threw her head back with her mirth, her shoulders shaking and her breasts bouncing as though to pop free from her tight bodice. The other two women wore red dresses, but Mary had on black, the color of mourning.

The waiters hovered near the piano by the kitchen door. Robert sat on the bench with his arms folded, his lower lip jutting as though he were a child rather than an eighteen-year-old young man. His Union uniform, blue with grass stains in the knees and arms, clashed with the immature pout.

Matthew stood over him, pointing at the tables. I chuckled; another argument about how Robert needed to prepare for the morning rush. I rolled my eyes. Good old Matthew, keeping everything perfect. Like usual, the tables were set with flowered dishes, polished silverware, and linen cloths. The chairs, with high backs and emerald cushions, were pushed in, and the tables had been spaced far enough apart to allow the ladies to fit their hoop skirts through the aisles. The light bulbs had been changed in the chandeliers and the portraits hanging on the walls had been dusted. A few other paintings remained in the cellar, safely hidden behind cardboard boxes and covered with tarps.

"Let Robert play," I called to Matthew. "He'll stop when the crowds come in." Parting the white lace curtains that hung over the front window, I peered at the street. A truck rumbled by with a faulty muffler, a woman walked her poodle along the sidewalk, and my husband headed up the tulip-lined path with a man.

Crap. I'd forgotten about his friend.

As Robert began a piece by Mozart, I opened the front door and grinned at the guests. "Good morning, gentlemen. How may we serve you?"

"This is Nigel." My husband clapped his friend on the shoulder. Nigel was taller by a foot, with cropped red hair and a hooked nose. Like my husband, Nigel wore jeans and a T-shirt.

He nodded. "Pleased to meet you, Mystic. I'm sorry I couldn't make the wedding last year."

"It must be nice to be visiting your parents." I leaned against the doorframe. When my husband and I first started dating, Nigel had already moved away. I only knew him from wild high school stories.

"I like traveling, but it does feel good to relax." Nigel stepped past me into the main dining room. "Tell me about your restaurant."

My husband pulled me against his chest to kiss my forehead. "Mystic took an old building and fixed everything up. New paint jobs. New roof."

"New veranda." I laughed. "Guests love eating outdoors in the nice weather." Nigel whistled, and I realized it might sound as if I had endless funds. "My dad owns a contracting business, so he and my brothers did the work. Carl and I live on the third floor."

"Which used to be the attic," my husband interjected. "The bedrooms have great sloped ceilings with skylights."

I beamed at Carl. "We also live on the second floor, but it has a great living room that I rent out for private parties. All of the furniture in there and down here are antiques from the 1800's. Most of the stuff was already here when we got the place, so my dad fixed them up, like that piano. Other items we got from antique dealers or they came as gifts. Some people just love cleaning out and don't mind giving stuff away so long as it reaches a good home."

"Civil War theme?" Nigel swept his hand at my staff in their old-fashioned garb.

"Welcome to the Yankee Inn." I lifted a vase off the nearest table and handed it to Nigel. "I found this in the cellar. I've found people don't usually associate this area with the Civil War, just because there weren't any major battles fought here, but families still sent loved ones off to fight. All of my workers dress like they did back then, speak like it, and…" I lifted my skirt and twirled. The hoop bumped my knees. "When you come in, it's like you stepped back in time. We pretend this is 1865."

"Interesting idea." Nigel handed the vase back.

"You should've seen how long Mystic worked on sewing this dress." Carl tugged on my puffed sleeve.

"You have an interesting name, too," Nigel said.

I shrugged. "My parents love the supernatural. So, who wants breakfast? My cook uses a recipe book from 1851. I found it in the cellar, too."

Mary waddled over with two menus. "Coffee or tea?"

The next morning, I had to sit down by ten o'clock. The Yankee Inn had only been open for two hours, but my back hurt and my stomach churned. Anne, my cook, passed me a cup of chamomile tea.

"I remember my first months. When you're in that special way, these spells can come at any time." She nodded at her twin daughters, the kitchen helpers. In their matching white dresses, the two little girls chopped vegetables at the counter.

"You mean I'll be this tired through all nine months?" I rubbed my stomach through my bodice. Soon, I'd have to wear modern maternity dresses, or sew a new gown.

"It'll be worth it."

I sipped the tea and the liquid scalded my tongue. I gasped, jerking back.

"Lay down for a while." Anne took the cup from my hands before I spilled it. "I'll send one of the girls to fetch you in thirty minutes."

I sighed, a headache pounding at the corners of my forehead. "Okay. I didn't feel this crappy yesterday." The staff did know what to do. In a year, we hadn't run across anything we couldn't handle. I slipped out the back door and up the narrow steps that had once been for servants. I continued to the top floor, working at the clasps on my dress to free myself from the confines, and froze in the hallway. Carl, Nigel, and a man holding a camcorder crouched in the hallway.

Nigel pointed at the bathroom door. "That's original, right, Carl?"

"One of the few," my husband said. "Mystic wanted to keep as many as she could because of the keyholes and doorknobs."

"They look cool," I interrupted. The three glanced at me. "What are you doing?"

"This is my cousin, Joel." Nigel clapped the shoulder of the man with the camcorder. "He's a paranormal investigator."

My heart thudded. "Wha-wh-why?" I always refused interviews. They could write about my brick building all they wanted, but I never let them in. I narrowed my eyes at Carl. "You let this guy up here?"

Carl kissed my sputtering lips. "Relax. Nigel thought this would be great for publicity."

I whirled away, but he grabbed my wrists. "Now, Mystic. Calm down."

I tried to pull free. "This is my business. You have your job at the mall. I don't need publicity." Tears burned my eyes. No, I wouldn't allow hormones to make me cry.

"Shh." He slid his hands up my arms to my shoulders and massaged the tight muscles. "Nigel asked if I'd do him this favor. They're only going to use a camcorder to film the building. I told them no EMF readers or a huge team, none of that stuff like on television."

"My name is Joel Puig." Nigel's cousin swung his camcorder lens in my direction. The black contraption was as small as his hand, with a red light on the front. "I've done this all my life, so you can trust my judgment. You're Mystic Jones McBride, age twenty-four and owner of the Yankee Inn?"

My body felt too numb to move. I wanted to rip his machine away and throw it down the stairs, but I could only nod, my dry lips parted.

"How did you acquire this building?"

I licked my lips. "P-please leave. I don't feel well." I pressed my hands over my stomach.

Carl continued to massage my shoulders. "Morning sickness again?" He had the decency to blush as he glanced at Joel and Nigel. "We better hurry this up. Mystic inherited this place from her great-aunt. The woman hadn't lived here since she was a teenager, but she got it from her parents and never sold it, said it had to stay in the family. Her kids live in California, but Mystic was in the area, so she won it."

Joel kept his camcorder held to his face, as though it were a deformed, metal growth. "City records show this was built in the year 1800 by Matthew Jones."

I nodded again. My long-lost relative – long lost, ha.

"He built it for his wife," Joel continued. They had only one surviving son, Matthew Junior. Matthew Senior died from a fall down the stairs. They thought his wife pushed him."

I wanted to say, "She did," but that would invite more questions. I leaned into Carl for his warmth. This couldn't be happening. Joel and Nigel needed to leave – now. They were going to ruin my business, my life.

"Matthew Junior's wife died of childbed fever," Joel said from behind his camcorder. "His three sons fought for the Union in the Civil War. The youngest, Robert, fled home. The neighbors hung him from the porch for being a deserter."

"He was a child," I murmured, although technically he was an adult at eighteen. Poor Robert. All he'd wanted to do was compose music, but his father sent him to war.

"The brother inherited the house and married a young woman named Anne. They had twin girls and a boy. Anne and the girls got sick with pneumonia. They died within a week." Joel lowered the camcorder enough to see me through both eyes. "You already know all this?"

I coughed to keep my voice light. "Of course. The family plot's in the backyard."

Joel nodded. "He remarried, this time a woman named Mary. She took in boarders. One girl arrived sick; spread the measles around the town. She died in a bed here. Another girl disappeared."

I rolled my eyes to pretend boredom. "It's all local legend. People wouldn't even come in here until I made it look presentable. They thought a ghost was going to snatch them up. Woohoo. Boo!" I wiggled my fingers.

"We're only here for proof," Nigel said. "This stuff is great."

"People died and you call it great?" Venom snapped in my voice and hormones brought fresh tears to my eyes.

Carl tightened his grip. "You should go to bed, honey. I'll help them finish up." He probably thought I was all riled up from the pregnancy – I was, sort of. I couldn't make him understand my real agitation without telling the truth.

"One more thing." Joel's smile made my throat tighten. "What happened to the girl who disappeared?"

Janice Boulanger. I pictured her standing beside the fireplace, laughing with Mary, as though she'd forgotten how the man she'd eloped with had murdered her. I squeezed my eyes shut, but a memory slipped into my mind: my dad, tearing up the attic floorboards, finding a human skeleton amongst rags.

"Lie down and I'll bring you some toast." Carl nudged me toward the bedroom. What if Carl discovered the secret of my staff? He never questioned why they hung around after hours. I ran the Inn and he lost himself in his office job.

I staggered past Joel and Nigel as though in a daze. What if Joel had photographs of the supposed ghosts? He might realize my staff looked identical to people who'd died in the building. I'd done such a good job of hiding their portraits in the cellar.

I sat on the foot of our canopy bed, remembering the first time I'd entered the kitchen with my mother. Anne and her two daughters had stood near the dusty table, staring at us with blank eyes.

"Oh my." Mom had laughed. "This place really is haunted."

Maybe it was wrong to use the ghosts for gain. I didn't have to pay them to work for me, so I could build up my funds. They enjoyed their jobs – they'd told me so. It gave them something to do. They got to interact with customers and no one knew enough to be scared. My ghosts had become costumed interpreters of the past.

I couldn't allow Joel to spoil the Yankee Inn.

Hurrying into the hallway, I found it empty. Carl's voice drifted from the stairs: "Mystic uses this for a sewing room."

I gripped the railing as I jogged down to them. Carl and Nigel admired the stained glass window my mom had made over my sewing machine.

Where's Joel?" My voice rasped.

"Downstairs." Carl frowned. "Darling, you need to rest."

No, not in the dining room! "In a second." My feet pounded against the stairs, my wide skirt brushing the wall. One sleeve slipped down my arm. I'd forgotten to refasten the top clasps on my bodice.

Two tables were occupied and Mary was seating a third couple. Robert still played the piano, with Matthew hovering over him. Anne would be in the kitchen with her girls, and—

Breath caught in my lungs. Joel stood near the front door filming Janice as she poured coffee for an elderly man.

I swept past the tables to grab Joel's arm. "I have to ask you to leave."

He shut off the camcorder, narrowing his eyes at me. "No one else knows your employees are dead."

My heart pounded so hard it ached. "Th-they aren't exactly dead."

"Janice Boulanger eloped when she was sixteen," he snapped. "Why does that girl, who I swear is sixteen, look exactly like a girl who disappeared in 1879?"

I gulped. "Weird coincidence. That doesn't prove anything."

Joel dropped his voice to a whisper: "I've been waiting for a long time to come in here. Janice Boulanger is my great-great-aunt. Her father told her not to marry the man. He was in the army, but he didn't seem honorable. Janice eloped anyway, but her father tracked them. She disappeared from here. I want to know what happened."

I drew a deep breath that rattled in my lungs. Joel's hands shook. I could help solve a family mystery.

"He killed her," I murmured. It wasn't my story, though, and maybe not my choice to make. I had only wanted to protect my friends.

"Janice." My voice wobbled. "Can you come here?"

She walked over, carrying the coffee pot. "Yes?"

I rubbed my forehead to ease the pounding. "This is Joel. He thinks you're his great-great-aunt. Do you want to talk to him? The second dining room isn't occupied yet."

"Oh. My." Janice wiped her free hand on her apron and plucked at a loose thread. "This way, please." She led Joel through a doorway.

I sat at the nearest table and sighed. What if he told everyone? Most wouldn't believe him, but some might and then what? Instead of customers, we've have gawking tourists. I knew my staff had to make their own choices, but they didn't know the first thing about the modern world – the television shows, documentaries, movies, walking tours. I needed to protect them from that exposure, at least.

My gaze fell on his camcorder. He'd set it on the table, probably in his shock over actually meeting Janice.

I glanced at the doorway, but didn't see them. The camcorder still required a tape in it, instead of a memory stick. I pressed rewind and held my breath until the tape stopped. Aiming the lens at the wall, I pressed the red record button.

the seventh step

by Terri Evert Karsten

It always rained on moving day. In the six times Arthur had moved since leaving his parents' house, through college dorms and apartments, not once had the day been dry. So he wasn't at all surprised when the sky loomed dark as he and his new bride, Betty, moved into the old house on 3rd Street. Arthur just hoped they could get most of the boxes inside before it started pouring.

The house had stood empty all winter. The realtor warned them mice or bats could have moved in, but the young couple didn't mind. They liked the gingerbread porch railings and quirky doorframes, and they figured they could chase away any pests that had found a way in.

Lightning crackled as Arthur began carrying his photographic equipment downstairs. No one had been down the basement steps for years. Tattered cobwebs curtained the wooden stairs and when Arthur pulled on the string of the bare bulb electric light hanging overhead, nothing happened.

Arthur replaced the light bulb and swept the steps clean, while Betty washed all the windows, inside and out, and began unpacking the kitchen

He had gone down the steps a dozen times, carrying the enlarger, trays for the chemical baths, and boxes of negatives, before he saw the little girl sitting there. He blinked. "Hello," he said. "What are you doing here?" He figured she must be a neighbor's child, coming over to see the newcomers.

"Waiting," she said. Her voice was wispy.

"Waiting? What for? I don't think the rain will stop anytime soon."

"You." She looked at him with sad, lonely eyes. "But I have to

95

wait a long time."

What an odd child, Arthur thought. Of course, he didn't have much experience with children. He and Betty were expecting their first at the end of the summer.

He stepped past her to set down his boxes. "You had better not wait there," he said over his shoulder. "I've got a lot to carry. You can wait upstairs in the kitchen."

When he turned to look again, the stairs were empty. The storm had moved past, and a brilliant shaft of sunlight streamed through the break in the clouds, lighting up the staircase through the open door. Dust motes danced in the light. Arthur stopped what he was doing to take a picture of the empty staircase. The composition was fascinating with jagged, open board steps zigzagging up the red brick wall.

Of course that was back before anyone used digital cameras, and Arthur never had switched even later when friends said it was easier to focus and less fuss. Arthur had always liked putzing in the darkroom, setting up his shot, and being surprised sometimes with the result.

This photograph certainly surprised him when he got around to printing it two months later. The light was just as he imagined, but there on the seventh step was the little girl, the one he had talked to that first afternoon. She appeared nearly translucent in the shot, with her knees hugged up under a diaphanous party dress, and a big bow holding back long ringlets perched on the top of her head. She wasn't looking at the camera, but just past it with a stare so intent he automatically glanced over his shoulder to see what was there.

He printed out a black and white glossy 8" x 10" and showed it to Betty to see if she recognized the child as one of the neighborhood kids. The photo had to be a double exposure. The film had not wound properly at the end of the roll. He had loaned the camera to his brother for a week or two, and maybe his brother had loaned it to a friend.

"I don't think she lives around here," Betty said. "My goodness, she looks as if she's right there, or maybe floating just a inch above the step. I wonder why she looks so sad!"

Arthur put the picture in his file, intending to ask his brother about the little girl the next time they came over. But with one thing and another, he forgot to ask and after awhile, he forgot about the picture too.

Arthur' and Betty's son, Douglas, was born at the end of August. From the first, he was a quiet child, and late to start real talking, though he often babbled nonsense. The doctor said there was nothing wrong with him; he was just a late-bloomer. Sure enough, by the time he was four, he had caught up to his cousins, but he still spent a good deal of time alone, talking to himself. He liked best to sit on the basement steps while Arthur was working.

"Who are you talking to?" Arthur asked him one day as he came up the steps.

"Sarah." The little boy stood up and took his father's hand. "She likes me. She said I'm the first one."

When Arthur told Betty about it, she wasn't worried. "Many children have imaginary friends." Her smile was reassuring. "He'll outgrow it."

Douglas never talked about Sarah after he started kindergarten. He played football in high school, and planned to study engineering after a stint in the army. The steps creaked in protest the day Douglas came downstairs to say good bye.

"I've got a couple hours before I have to leave," he said. "You want some help with anything?"

Father and son had worked together many times before. That day, Arthur was sorting some of his old prints to see what was worth saving. Douglas took one of the files. "Hey, these are from the first year you moved here," he said, shuffling through the folder of 8" x10" glossy photos. He pulled out the picture of the little girl on the steps. "I remember her," he said with a smile. "Didn't I play with her before I started school?"

Arthur took the picture and stared at it. Douglas must have seen the picture when he was little and used the image to create his imaginary friend. Arthur smiled at the memory.

Six months later they were notified Douglas had been killed in Iraq. The whole house seemed to sigh as Arthur and Betty clung to each other and wept.

Betty never recovered from the loss of her son. She hung pictures of him in every room, and talked as if he were coming home on the weekend. She made scrapbooks of his schoolwork and classmates, saying how thrilled he would be to see them all. She found the picture of the little girl on the steps and had it framed.

"You told me we didn't even know her," Arthur protested.

"Nonsense," Betty responded, wiping away imaginary smudges on the glass. "She was Douglas' first friend."

She hung the picture on the wall in the dining room, next to the picture of Douglas smiling shyly on his first day of school.

Years passed. Every Saturday when Arthur walked down the steps to his darkroom, the seventh step creaked, almost like the sigh of a sad little girl. Arthur left all the pictures on the wall even after Betty died. His world shrank and grew silent. Friends drifted away or died after he retired, and when his brother went into the nursing home, it was too far away to visit. Some weeks he went days without talking to anyone other than a nod to the paper boy if he was up early enough or a greeting to the cashier as he limped past the register at the grocery store.

It became harder to go up and down the basement stairs, but he kept up the old habit. He would shoot a roll of film one day, and develop it the next, even when he had to stop and lean on the wall to catch his breath.

As the quiet around him grew, Arthur became lonely. He took to talking to the picture of the little girl and he could imagine her listening and nodding.

Then there came a day like that day so long ago when the sun filtered through the dust motes down the basement steps. He had come down early in the morning, slowly and methodically fixing and drying his prints, making a proof sheet. He had to stop often to sit on the stool and sip his cold coffee. But now the coffee was gone and the basement had turned frigid.

Arthur was tired. Too tired. He stopped at the bottom of the stairs, heart pounding as if he had run a mile. He couldn't seem to catch his breath. With one hand on the wall, he stepped up with his right foot, and dragged the left to rest beside it. 15 steps to the top. He would never make it.

He looked up. There sitting on the 7th step was the little girl, the same one he had photographed so long ago. Her expression was solemn but no longer sad. She looked right into his eyes and held out a hand.

"Hello, Arthur." She smiled. "I've been waiting for you."

a night of storm and shadows

by John Michaels

Thunder grumbled along the ridge tops as I sprinted across the street to the old church on the corner. I'd have to hurry if I had any hope of finishing up in there before the storm hit. It was my job to lock up by 10:00, and I was running late.

Leaving my friends behind every night at the pool hall was not my idea of a good job, but with tuition, books and three square meals to pay for, I took on anything that gave me a little more cash. And it didn't seem so bad when I started. I just had to make sure the place was empty, switch off the lights, and lock the doors. An easy $5 for 15 minutes' work.

The trouble was, the place gave me the creeps. The church had to be more than a hundred years old. It was roughly T-shaped, with a number of extra rooms jutting out here and there like knobs. The massive walls had been built with local limestone, and decorated with carved limestone and archways. A bell tower in the style of the old world cathedrals pierced the sky, making the church visible for miles. The place dominated the center of town and attracted visitors from all over to admire the architecture. But no matter how empty it was when I arrived, I never could quite shake the feeling someone was in there, looking over my shoulder, watching me, and waiting.

Rain spattered the parking lot as I ducked inside the back door. I paused to catch my breath. Suddenly an old man stepped out from beside the curtains, any sound of his movement covered by the ominous thunder. He was dressed in faded denims and a plaid shirt that could have been my grandfather's.

I must have gasped because the guy chuckled, a grating hollow sound in the empty vestibule. There was no humor in it, only menace; as if he wanted something I couldn't give.

"Caught you coming late," he grumped. "When I had the job, I would have died before anyone found me shirking."

"Look, mister," I said, trying to calm my racing heart. He was just some old crazy that came in off the street, maybe looking for a place to shelter out of the rain. "I've got to lock up now. The church is closing." I didn't much like kicking him out like this, but he couldn't stay in the church overnight.

I pulled off my backpack to reach inside for the keys.

"I know this job better than you do," the old guy muttered. "Fifty years at it and never once late."

The door creaked. When I looked up the guy was gone.

A sudden gust of wind caught the door and slammed it wide open. Outside leaves swirled in a dust devil. The old guy must have been faster than he looked because the courtyard was empty.

"Okay," I said, feeling anything but okay. I closed the door.

Lightning flashed, and the curtains in the vestibule window billowed toward me like a pair of drunken ghosts. I slammed the window shut. In the sudden hush, I could heard rain pelting the eaves, and something else, like a sigh, as if the building itself were exhaling. Making sure the door had latched, I turned the key in the lock, heard the click of the tumbler, and headed downstairs to the basement.

I switched on my flashlight since the stairwell was unlit. In the hallway below, florescent bulbs in dusty fixtures shaped more shadow than light. I had to walk through each corridor of class-rooms and store rooms as the storm battered the church outside. Down here, in this windowless maze, I could no longer hear the thunder or see the lightning, but I could feel the electric charge in the air and the hairs on my arm crackled with static. The musty smell of an old basement in summer curled around my nostrils, and my footsteps echoed on the tiles down the long hallway.

Or was it really my own footsteps I heard? I stopped and a half beat later the soft shuffling I took for an echo stopped too. Some-one was there. I could feel them. I took another step and two steps sounded behind me. One of my friends, I thought sourly, coming to tease me. I spun around back toward the stairs, shouting, "I see you, Karl!"

But there was no one there.

I hurried though the rest of the basement, checking each door to see it was locked. Soft footfalls mocked my every step, but I saw no one. At the far end of the basement I flicked off the hall lights and the feeling someone followed me grew stronger.

Back upstairs I locked the kitchen door and the great hall. The floors creaked while the wind outside battered the stone walls as if a thousand silent voices demanded entry. "That's crazy thinking." I tried to shake off the fear. "You're going to end up as bonkers as that old man," I told myself and hurried on to finish the job. I had only the sanctuary left, one door on the side, and the main door at the entrance.

Even as late as it was, I half expected to see someone still in the church, so strong was the feeling I was not alone. But the place was just as empty as the basement had been. After locking the side door, I stood for a moment in the archway, trying to slow the unreasonable pounding of my heart. The sanctuary was long and narrow, but well lit, with ornate lamps hanging from the vaulted ceiling beams casting shadows on the low backed wooden pews flanking either side of the center aisle. Tall stained glass windows lined both walls and light from the streetlights outside dimly shone through, reflecting eerie blue and red pools of light on the marbled floor.

The storm had intensified while I was downstairs. Thunder rumbled deep across the sky and bursts of lightning flashes charged the air. Rain pelted the glass like tiny stones. The bare tree branches silhouetted black against the stained glass whipped and strained at their moorings in a macabre dance, as if they meant to take off swirling into the night like so many bats.

And someone was watching me.

I couldn't see anyone, but I could feel his eyes on me. I took a deep breath and stepped out of the shadows. The last door was at the far end of the church. At that moment, lightning flared in a brilliant crash and the lights went out.

I fumbled for the flashlight, pressing the switch with shaking hands. Swinging the light frantically back and forth, I started down the center aisle of the church. Shuffling footsteps followed. Again I turned, waving the light behind me towards the darkened corners, the stairwell and even the ceiling. The beam pierced the blackness, lighting empty steps, a cushion askew on the bench, the tarnished edge of the window frame. From outside I heard a loose shutter banging in the wind.

Then I felt a cold breath on the back of my neck.

Shrieking in fear, I whirled to face it. Something ducked between my legs and I tripped, sprawling into the nearest pew and crashing to the floor. The flashlight flew out of my hand and blinked off. I heard it roll a few feet and bump something hard. Then silence.

I scrambled up on hands and knees, groping blindly for the light. How far had it rolled?

A hollow chuckle filled the darkness. Behind me? In front? I froze like a rabbit caught in the headlights.

Then I felt a cold hand on my shoulder and someone pressing the flashlight into my grip.

"You ought to be more careful," a gruff voice tickled my ear. "Do the job right or don't do it at all."

I shoved the switch forward and the beam of light burst forth, but the sanctuary was empty.

I ran. Down the long aisle out the front door, plunging into the driving rain. The hollow ghostly laugh followed me all the way.

The next day I quit. If that old guy wanted his job back so much, he could have it.

shadow

by Hannah Jones

Mat's shadow went everywhere with him. Wherever his eight-year-old routine took him, he was sure to glance down and see the black blot nipping at his heels: at the bus stop, in the school lunch line, even in the bathroom. It was clingy and insecure, always mirroring him in his every movement and trying to replicate his size and shape. It often failed, warping Mat's silhouette to tall, stringy proportions with spindly sticks for arms and legs. He had tried on several occasions to shake it, jumping as high as he could in an attempt to snap their connection like a rubber band, or running as fast as his young legs could take him in an effort to leave it in his dust. It stayed resolutely fastened to him, however. He'd sooner succeed in unlatching his own feet than succeed in abandoning his shadow. This bothered him sometimes, but not as much as green beans or math homework.

He was noticing his silent copycat on that particular day as he traipsed along the damp, overgrown fields behind his parents' house. It was a dark blue-gray that early afternoon, starkly contrasting with the long, straw-colored grass under his wet sneakers. Mat's father had told him that the entire area had been farmland once, but now, shaggy and abandoned, it served only as a massive condominium for bugs and the occasional gopher. Having moved into the house only a few days before, the boy had taken it upon himself to learn the contours and crannies of his barren backyard. His parents weren't as interested in what lay in the emptiness. His mother would glance out the sliding glass door, sigh, and mutter, "It all looks rather depressing, doesn't it? Just a big, weedy pancake."

"Maybe a big deck, or a pool," his father would mumble. "Yes, a pool… got to look into that sometime."

The boy then set down his crayon and sought to take rein of the conversation. "I found a rabbit warren," he chirped.

"Are we allowed to build a pool?" his mother asked.

"Just yesterday. It's a big one, with kits," he continued.

"I'll look into it," his father muttered into his paper.

"Can I take them some carrots, please?" Mat asked.

"Oh, honey, no," his mother answered, turning away from the sliding glass door. "Don't feed them, whatever you do."

His young brow furrowed. "Why not?" he asked. He glanced at his drawing, three brown rabbits with a pile of bright orange carrots.

His mother turned back to the glass. "Because they'll follow you home."

Mat stopped short, and his shadow froze behind him. His sandy head turned left, then right, scanning the rustling yellow sea. He turned his gaze to his feet, facing his indigo outline.

"Was that you?" he asked. The shadow did not reply, but shrugged when Mat did. The boy was about to continue on his way when suddenly, out of the rasp of the grass, he heard what had given him pause once again: a hum. Not like a bumblebee, but like his mother brushing her hair. It was a musical hum, quiet but clear. Mat checked his shadow again just to be sure before calling, "Hello?"

The hum stopped short. He immediately regretted having said anything, as if his acknowledgement of the noise had killed it, but to his surprise, he was answered.

"Hello."

He felt his heart quicken, his little palms sweating. "Hello!" he yelled, whipping his gaze in a circle around him. "Hello! Is someone there? I can't see you!"

The voice floated toward him again, thin as his shadow. "Hello! I'm here! I'm here!"

Mat bounded toward the source of the sound, straining against the moan of the wind to hear it. "Where?" he shouted. His eye caught a dark blotch in the grass unlike his own, and he stopped. There, in the midst of the weeds and gravel, lay a square frame made of old, rotted boards. The center was an abyss so black, it was as unfathomable as a pool of ink.

"Down here!" the voice echoed up to him.

Mat knelt next to the hole, staring blindly into it. His parents had never mentioned a well on the property. Its profile was so well hidden among the gangly yellow fauna that he supposed they had never seen it. Neither had, apparently, the high voice that yelped to him now. "Are you all right?" he asked. His words tumbled and bounced off the sides of the cavernous depths, falling forever into the blackness. The distance, unseen but not unfelt, frightened him.

"I think so," the voice answered. True to form, the person in the well did not sound pained. The voice rang like a little bell in the gloom, unlabored and even lighthearted. It was a girl's voice, he thought, perhaps a child his age. He noticed for the first time a ratty rope that trailed out of the mouth of the well, secured on a spike driven into one of the boards.

"Do you need some help?" he asked, taking the line in his hands. "There's a rope here, so maybe I can pull you up."

There was a pause from the well's interior, then a soft tug from the other end of the rope, pulling gently against his grip.

"This one?" the voice asked.

"That's the one!" Mat cried. "Just hold on and I'll lift you out!" He was ecstatic. Finding a warren of rabbits was one thing, but this was a real live person he had discovered in his backyard. He seized the line and yanked it backward, hand over hand, piling the coils behind him. There was a hollow scraping noise rising out of the ink, and it grew progressively louder as he heaved. Sweat beaded on his forehead as he pulled through the home stretch, pulling his catch over the decrepit rim of the well. He nearly dropped it back in again.

The rope was tied onto the handle of an ancient looking bucket, which was most likely what was making the racket in the darkness. Sitting in the mouth of the rusty old thing was a young girl in a sopping, filthy dress.

Her skin was a pale, blue-violet tinged with a pearly gray. Her hair, soaked and tangled, fell in a ratty black curtain to the small of her back. Her right leg was a thin, atrophied shaft in a droopy stocking. Her left leg bent in the wrong direction. Her hands, which she held politely folded in her dirty lap, had eight fingers between them and none of them seemed to agree on which crooked, unnatural angle to point. Her eyes were brown and bloodshot, tinted the same color as the grass at the edges. She smiled a smile of broken, jagged teeth and blue gums.

"Thank you," she said pleasantly.

"...Don't mention it," was all that the boy could think to say.

A silence suffocated the next two seconds before he added, "Um... Are you sure you're all right?"

"Oh, never better," she said, rising awkwardly on her one good leg.

The bucket, free of its cargo, was brimming with murky water, which Mat realized had been the only weight he had been hauling to the surface. The girl was easily his size, and weighed absolutely nothing. Her twisted fingers plucked at the hem of her dress, as if any amount of preening was going to fix the ruined fabric.

"What's your name?" she asked, glancing up through her hair. The boy was apprehensive, but confronted with her simple cordiality, he felt unable to refuse her an answer. "Mat," he replied.

She grinned, her maw a jagged purple mess. "Mat," she repeated. "I like that name. I'm Eunice. I'm not too fond of it- my name, I mean."

The boy shrugged shakily. "I think it's all right," he whispered.

"Really?" Eunice asked. "You can't mean it. It's such an ugly name. Yoo-niss. I've always wanted to be named Calliope. Much prettier."

"I don't know about that," Mat breathed, turning his eyes to his feet. His shadow, ever present, stared back at him. The blue reminded him of the edges of Eunice's lips. "I should be going," he said, not daring to turn his eyes up again.

"So soon?" Eunice asked, disappointment ringing through her silver bell voice. "We've only just met. Did I say something?"

"No. My Mom. She'll worry. Bye, now." He turned then and

began to walk, his stare locked into the ground. After about five strides, he broke into a run. His legs pounded against the dirt, and yellow grass slapped into his knees only to be parted by the force of his step. He counted thirty seconds before he allowed himself to look over his shoulder.

She was twenty feet away, her black hair clearly visible against the clear sky, hobbling slowly in his direction. He squeezed his eyes shut and ran even harder.

His parents commented little on his lack of appetite and his unnatural quiet that evening at dinner. His mother thought he might be sick and proposed an earlier bedtime. Mat surprised her when he didn't argue, instead placing his half-eaten plate by the sink and ascending the stairs to his room. By the time he had donned his Batman pajamas, he had convinced himself that it had all been a product of his imagination; Eunice, the well, the soft melody that had called to him like a siren. It was all a daydream, he reasoned, climbing under the covers. His shadow pressed against him as he laid his head on the pillow, his rosy cheek embracing its dark profile. He thought about rabbits until he was finally able to close his eyes and drift off to sleep.

In his dreams, he was attempting to outrun his shadow as he darted across the yellow field. As usual, he could not free himself of his twin, but in his unconscious mind the shadow grew heavier and heavier, weighing him down and eventually forcing him to drag it along like a ball and chain. It even clinked like iron shackles as he strained, sweat beading in a familiar pattern on his forehead. *Clink. Clink. Clink.* Every step. Every breath.

"Leave me alone!"

Clink.

Mat's lungs seized and his eyes shot open. The sky was obsidian outside his window, cloud cover rendering it starless and moonless. His body lay tangled in his bed sheets, damp and sore, and his heart fluttered sickeningly against his rib cage. He held his breath, waiting. Had he heard…?

Clink.

He threw the covers off of his body and staggered out of bed. His parents' snores resonated softly from their room, both his father's bass and his mother's alto. They were both fast asleep. So the noise couldn't have been either of them.

Clink.

He stopped at the top of the stairs, gawking down into the kitchen. There she was, sitting atop the very chair in which he had picked at his dinner, her twisted leg hanging awkwardly off to the side. The kitchen table was littered with a random assortment of foodstuffs, to which Eunice was happily helping herself. A package of Wonder bread was sitting ravaged and crumbstrewn to her left, keeping the company of a jar of horseradish and a peach with a single bite torn from the flesh. Cups of milk, half-consumed and neglected, were scattered throughout a minefield of forks and knives. The pale, broken child was currently occupied with a teaspoon, which she regularly dipped into a jar of honey and scooped golden stickiness into her mouth.

Clink went the metal against the glass.

She turned her head and her yellow-rimmed eyes met his. Mat's fluttery heart stopped for an instant. She smiled, and a driblet of saliva and honey trailed out of her mouth and down her jaw.

"Hello, Mat," she said, her words mucked and comically slurred. She seemed to realize what a sty she had made of the table and herself, and ducked her head with a giggle. "I hope you don't mind. I was just so hungry. I haven't eaten in ages."

"…Ages," Mat rasped. His throat felt like sandpaper.

"I must say, you have a wonderful house," she said, regarding the dim kitchen. "I've never been in a place quite so fancy. Where does your father work? Is he a doctor?"

"You can't be here," the boy said. The words left his mouth before he could stop them. "You can't come in my house. You've got to leave." He watched the girl's face, waiting for her to react. A golden gob of sweetness fell slowly, silently, from her lips, and her jaundiced eyes did not blink. After what seemed like an age in itself, she gently set the jar on the table, patting it with her mangled hand, and spoke in her lovely, chiming voice.

"Mat," she began. "Have you ever been lonely?"

Mat didn't answer. His hand found the railing and gripped it for support.

"I have felt very lonely for a very long time," she continued, taking in stride his silence. "But you have shown me such kindness, Mat. I thought after today… I wouldn't have to feel so terribly lonely again." She lifted herself off the chair, standing on her good leg. "And neither would you."

Mat backed away from the stairwell, his shadow quivering on the wall beside him. "Mom," he whispered. "Dad." His voice would not obey him, producing only wispy exhales when he wanted to scream. From the landing below, he could hear a sugary sweet melody rising toward him. Silver bells and honey humming in the stillness. "Mom… Dad…"

Thump.

Eunice's one good leg had found the bottom stair. The step creaked with the shifting of her weight, followed closely with her next step.

Thump. Creak. Thump.

"Mommy…" Mat's voice was just a faint mewl in the deserted hallway. The song was getting louder, now, stronger with every step.

Thump. Creak. Thump.

Mat and his shadow bolted, sprinting back to his room. He dove to the floor and thrust his arms under his bed, digging furiously.

Thump. Creak. Thump.

"Mat…"

He tossed aside a yo-yo, several comic books, and a stuffed dinosaur. His forehead was dripping, and his lungs felt aflame.

"Mat, I…"

He looked over his shoulder and saw her, her skin swollen and blue in the midnight darkness. She lurched forward, humming, smiling, dripping golden saliva.

"…I want…"

He overturned an entire toy box, his breath burning and condensing into rhythmic whimpers.

"*...To be...*"

The air stank of honey and rot. Her crooked fingers were reaching out even as his groped frantically in the blackness.

"*...With you...*"

His hand wrapped around a cylinder of plastic.

"*...FOREVER.*"

He withdrew his flashlight from the fathoms of his bed and whirled to face her, inches away from him, shaded dark in his shadow. Her teeth, her eyes, the purple, blue, yellow, sick, warped, dead. He flipped the switch and cringed in a silent scream as he threw the artificial light at her with all his might. "Leave me alone!"

"Are you sure you're feeling all right? You seemed so out of it last night."

Mat tried to smile at his mother, holding a crayon gingerly in his hand.

"I'm all right. Now," he said.

His father crossed his arms, his forehead creased in worry. "What was with the huge mess on the table this morning, kiddo?" he asked. "Crumbs everywhere, milk left out, nearly everything sticky. Did you get hungry?"

Mat shrugged. "Sorry about that," was all he said.

His parents glanced at one another, considering. They were still fretting, he could tell.

"I think a pool would be fun to have," he said. "In the backyard, I mean."

They seemed to lighten up a little, smiling in relief at the childish desire he expressed to them.

"Well, it looks like that may be in the cards," his father said. "I'll look into it."

His mother rolled her eyes, smiling. "It's almost time to get to school," she said. "Grab your backpack, and let's get going."

"Okay," Mat replied, standing. He crossed the kitchen floor, passing through splashes of sunlight from the sliding glass door, his shadow trailing behind him.

His mother blinked, perplexed, as he climbed the stairs and disappeared into the hall. It must have been her eyes playing tricks on her, she thought. But, for a single second, she could have sworn that her son's shadow was moving in a way unlike his own; almost as if it were limping.

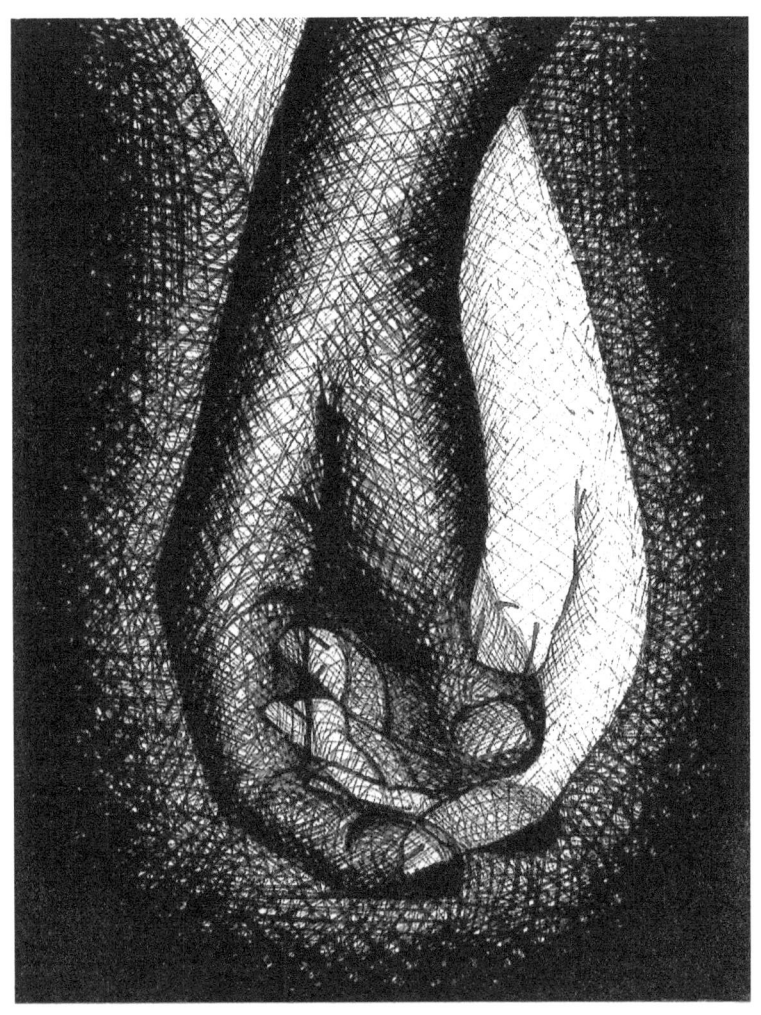

walk me to class?

by N. R. Mehlhoff

I have seen many strange events around the eerie town of Winona. I have seen men kill themselves to be among their ghost lovers and I have heard of students dying in the morning before class or students taking their own lives in the depths of the bluffs surrounding the town. The tale I am about to tell outweighs all fears, whether real or imagined.

It was late into the night of April 10th or early morning April 11th I suppose. I had left my apartment to go on a walk. I could not sleep and sauntering about in the cloudy, cool twilight seemed oddly appealing. It had been a warm and humid spring day with tornado watches and nasty gusts of wind which should have forewarned for the storm to come.

It must have been 2:48 am when I began walking back across the Winona State campus towards my apartment on the other side of town. The campus seemed to be entirely vacant, not surprising for a Sunday night. I cut across the sidewalks, smoking my last cigarette. The courtyard was so serene and yet eerie as if there was not a soul awake, but the wind was still blowing. It howled between the buildings and shook the trees. I stopped and stood in a patch of grass right near the middle of the courtyard. I inhaled through my cigarette. I held it, then exhaled and a furious gust of wind blew over the buildings and through the courtyards and immediately the smoke was gone, blown and dispersed through the courtyard.

As that gust blew away a sudden flurry of commotion came from all around. Footsteps after footsteps upon more footsteps, hustling around, and with the steps came voices, whispering, talking, and muttering. I glanced around and then I saw them: phantoms, dark figures, people in the shadows and the dark, coming out of all the buildings, coming out of the doors, all at once, in the same way students do during the day after classes are over. No lights were on in the buildings and at this time of night all the doors to all the buildings were locked. The people rushed the sidewalks of the campus courtyard. I cannot express my confusion. My first thought was that it was some student protest or activism to promote some sort of equality or justice. But there was something still eerie about all the people. Most of them looked foreign, not foreign of space but of time. Their styles were so much different than this time period and it was so authentic I could not doubt it. Some of them were wearing flat caps and others wearing suits; some girls strolled in summer dresses with ribbons in their hair; some people clearly came of a certain era; most of them were without backpacks. Once in a while one would pass that looked of this time but it was rare. They talked to each other as most students do between passing but not joyously, not loudly, and certainly not smiling. They were muttering and whispering among themselves, all with solemn lost and grave expressions.

I stood in the grass for quite a few minutes confounded by the event before me. No one seemed to notice me. No one so much as glanced at me, even the ones who walked through the grass. A few girls sat down in a circle just three feet from me. I stood there. I'd say scared stiff, but I wasn't scared, just simply stiff. I stared down at them. They were wearing tye-dyed shirts and jeans, some cut off, some baggy towards the ankles, some sandals, some bare foot. I watched as one girl lit a smoke and held it between two fingers as she took a drag.

"Excuse me, what's going on? Why are all these students here?" I asked.

They didn't answer me, didn't even turn.

"Excuse me." I took a half step and leaned towards them. I paused.

No answer.

"Excuse me!"

No answer. Not a glance.

I turned then to the passing crowd, milling that way and this way and I said to them, "Hey!"

I paused. "Hello! What's going on?"

It was then that I noticed a man I had not noticed before. He came from across a sidewalk, probably from a bench beside a building. He was looking at me with the most extreme concern on his face. I was stiff again, frozen staring at this man with relief. He was a middle-aged man with a large beard and ragged clothes. He crossed the sidewalk and nudged people aside to be able to pass. The people walked around him, but they didn't seem to actually notice him.

The man walked up to me, stopping a few paces ahead of me. He stood there studying, looking me up and down. "What are you doing here?" he said. The question seemed almost insulting.

"I was just walking through campus. Who are these people?"

"So you can see them?" he asked.

"What do you mean? There are hundreds of them!" I said throwing my arms out and turning my head.

"Not everyone can see them," he said. He looked at me very plainly and put his hands in his pants pockets. "And they cannot see you. Most of them can't anyways."

"So... what? They're ghosts?"

"They're students," he said. "They all go to school here. Class has just let out and the students are hustling to their next class or perhaps going home."

"It's three in the morning," I interrupted.

"No, it's almost three," he said. He looked down at the ground and rustled the grass with his shoe. "When I was in my third year here, she had to go up to Lake City for a film project. She asked me to go with her. It would only take about an hour, she told me. But it was a Thursday and my buddies were going out to a party. She told me to go out and I would see her soon. I told her I loved her. She parked her car on highway 61, on the side farthest from the river. She crossed the road and was hit and killed by a drunk driver speeding around the corner before she even made it to the other lane."

I didn't know what to say. His story had only added to my confusion.

"They appear whenever the weather is bad and I am always here. It's why I still live in Winona, working one job or another; because I can't leave her. I discovered them roughly a year after she died. I was scared to death and my heart jumped when she came out." He pointed at a beautiful young blonde girl walking down the sidewalk with a smile on her face and a large camera hanging around her neck. "She is always late for class because she takes pictures of anything and everything. She has always found beauty in everything. I've been here ever since. She tells me to go out and that I'll see her soon and I tell her I love her."

"Now then," he said smiling, "I have to go see my girl, but I am sure I will see you again." He walked to the sidewalk and took the girl's hand in his. She didn't pay attention to me if she had seen me.

"Hey," I exclaimed, "But why can I see them?"

"You'll see her," he said walking down the sidewalk with his girl. "Or rather, she'll see you."

I stood and searched through the faces as they hustled by still in a state of disbelief, and without a clue of what or who I was looking for. Then I saw her walking towards me from the left, a young girl with glasses and shimmering brown hair. She saw me and stopped walking, as shocked to see me and I was to see her.

She had died my second year here, a freshman in my biology class. We had quickly become study buddies. She had a crush on me I could tell. When she passed away, ironically my own heart was broken. I regretted never allowing her to love me. I had made up excuses not to hang out with her outside of studying. She was a sweet and funny girl and I think I had always secretly admired her. After biology, she would always ask me to walk her to her next class and I always would. I always loved the conversations we had on that walk.

She died unexpectedly one morning before class about a year ago. I had expected to see her at biology, but she didn't show up. Now we stood ten yards apart, both stunned by the other's appearance or even existence. Smiles slowly grew on our faces as we started to understand.

"Walk me to class?" she asked. I walked towards her and held out my hand. She took it in hers and then pulled me in and hugged me, desperately, lonesomely. She was cold to the touch. She embraced me tightly and I heard her sob on my shoulder and I held her tightly.

We walked to her next class hand in hand and we had the best conversation we had ever had. I walked her right up to her classroom which I had never done before. She asked me if she would see me again and I told her she would. She gave me a quick hug and then her hand slipped out of mine as she walked into the classroom. As she walked into the classroom, I saw the room full of other students and a professor standing at the front of the room.

The door closed and I stood there, still in disbelief of the whole night, still stiff. I didn't want to leave, but I didn't know what to do at this point. Without any clear idea in my head, I reached forward for the door handle, but I couldn't turn it. The door was locked as it should be at three in the morning. I walked home by the most roundabout way possible trying to comprehend everything I had seen and trying to decide if I was crazy or if the night's events had truly taken place. For the longest time, I disregarded the entire night. I never told a soul of that night and I started to believe it had never happened.

Weeks later, on May 1st, I woke up to a thunderstorm. I looked at the clock and saw it was 2:37 am. I immediately jumped from my bed and changed into clothes. I grabbed my jacket and walked out into the pouring rain and fierce winds. I walked the six blocks to campus. I walked past the library and into the middle of campus. The rain had reduced to only a cold mist. It was 2:48 and students were beginning to trickle out of their classes. It was all real. The sensation running through my body was intoxicating. I was standing in a world outside of my own. I hurried across campus to the science building, passing students and the herds crowded the sidewalks. None of them saw me.

I reached the front door of Stark Hall just as some students were coming out. The door closed behind them and I grabbed the handle but it was locked. I would have to wait for her. I turned around and searched through the students. I saw the middle aged man walking hand in hand with the blonde haired girl.

"Walk me to class?" I heard a voice from behind me say.

"Absolutely," I told her.

And so each night when the weather is bad, when the wind is blowing, when the rain is coming down, when all my friends are staying inside, I go out for a walk so that I can walk her to class, so that she knows that I am there and she is in my mind. And the students walk all around us because they came to this university to learn, to be among friends, to find a place that they belong, and to fall in love, and death isn't going to stop them.

hearse haunting

by Terri Evert Karsten

Roscoe didn't much mind his new job driving the hearse, except when his passengers were reluctant to leave.

Working for Hanrahan's Funeral Parlor was Roscoe's fifth job since leaving school, but it was the first job where no one gave him odd looks for talking to himself, if only because not many people heard him while he was driving. The worst job had been at the convenience shop near the Safeway grocery. A pair of old ladies had complained to the manager and he'd been sacked not quite two hours after starting. All he'd done was ask one lady to move her shopping cart off the chimney sweep's toes. Was it his fault no one else could see the sweep? The poor kid had come in for a break from the wind, wind being a terrible trial for the ephemerals, as Roscoe liked to call them. They always moaned that the wind could blow them willy-nilly across the countryside, and Roscoe had to admit they had a legitimate gripe.

Before the convenience store, he had worked two full weeks stocking shelves at the Fleet Farm warehouse before one of the other workers told the boss that Roscoe was just too weird to work around.

"He talks to the empty air, like there's someone right in front of him," Bob complained. "He keeps stopping the forklift in the middle of the aisle."

Roscoe smiled ruefully. All he had done was let the duck hunters cross. They had been out in the Armistice Day Storm years ago, and were still trying to warm up. They came in every time it rained, trailing bits of duckweed and drifting like smoke. Not that getting run over by the forklift hurt, they assured Roscoe, but it did make them feel sort of scattered. Roscoe figured it didn't take all that long to let them cross, and if it gave them a bit of comfort,

125

then it was time well spent. Trouble was, the boss had not understood that Roscoe just wanted to help out. He gave him the last day's pay and told him not to come back.

So all in all, landing the job at Hanrahan's was lucky. No one complained about Roscoe's conversations, and really, he ended up listening a lot more than talking. Most folks just wanted a last chance to tell a story or two before fading. Nettie Pullman confessed she had been stealing her neighbor's daffodils for years because the neighbor's tree shaded Nettie's yard. Young Darryl Applebee revealed how he had been the one throwing spitballs in Ms. Nelson's math class, not Tommy Makrel. Darryl laughed so hard he faded before the hearse even entered the cemetery gates. Naturally, Roscoe worried about these confessions. He wanted to make things right, but what could he do? It's not like he could give back the daffodils or take away Tommy's detentions. No one would believe him anyway. So he just listened, never revealing what the folks told him, and their secrets were buried with them.

Of course, not all the folk Roscoe delivered to their final rest had something to say, but most did. So when Max Cunningham was loaded into the back of the hearse, Roscoe was not surprised to feel a tap on his shoulder before they had even pulled away from the church.

Max had been mayor of the town for 30 years before he retired. A tall man, mostly bald, he had grown rounder in his later years, but no less exuberant. He'd been playing golf when he keeled over from a heart attack. His wife had died ten years earlier and both daughters had moved out of state, but Max was well liked around town, so the church was crowded on the day of the funeral.

Roscoe waited in the hearse with the wipers on while the pallbearers loaded the casket. He gave the mourners time to make their way through the drizzle to their own parked cars before leading the procession out of town. That's when he felt Max tap his shoulder.

"Would you look at that?" Max said.

Roscoe glanced in the rearview mirror.

Max sat half out of the coffin, a fresh, red carnation stuck in his pocket. "Must be the whole town following us. I always did love a parade."

Roscoe smiled. A lot of folks liked this part and counted just how many came to the funeral. "It's a great turnout, Mayor, but you've had plenty of fame before now, haven't you?" he said.

"You got that right, boy. Why do you think they call it the Max C. Mall?"

It took thirty minutes to drive to the cemetery and Max spent the whole of it regaling Roscoe with stories of his good deeds and great friends. That surprised Roscoe since most folks talked about their regrets, but he just let Max go on, figuring it was his last chance to say whatever he needed to say.

Glencoe Cemetery graced the top of a hill, with huge arbor-vitae trees planted a century ago offering shelter from the wind. Roscoe parked the hearse and turned back to wave to Max as the pallbearers took out the casket.

The six men shouldered their burden and trudged toward the open grave, but Max stayed put in the back of the hearse. "It's too wet to get out," he complained.

"You'll rest easier now," Roscoe encouraged. "Never mind the rain." He'd had enough experience with ephemerals to know that folks who didn't leave with their casket were apt to turn wispy and scattered before fading

"Rest? What do I want with resting?" Max scoffed. "I've never rested a day in my life." He floated over the seat back to sit beside Roscoe up front. Together they watched the mourners surround the grave. The preacher's words drifted toward the hearse in disconnected bits and pieces. Max and Roscoe sat in silence until the crowd dribbled away. The last to leave were Max's daughters, their cheeks wet with tears and rain. "Good girls," Max said, his voice a bit gruff.

Finally the cemetery was empty, and Max still sat in the front seat, his happy smile from earlier giving way to a glum look.

"I gotta be driving back now, " Roscoe said after a long pause.

"Well, don't let me stop you." Max bent his head to rest on his hands in an attitude of total dejection.

"Maybe you ought to …go on," Roscoe encouraged.

"I can't." Max slowly shook his head without looking up.

"I'm not finished yet."

"You're dead," Roscoe said. He hated being so blunt, but some folks needed a little help. "That's about as finished as a body can get. What more can you do?" He started the engine, hoping Max would take the hint. Roscoe's boss would be steaming mad if he didn't get the hearse back soon.

Max still hadn't moved. "All those people," he moaned. "All mourning for me."

He sure enough had the moaning part of being dead figured out, Roscoe decided. Now if he could just accept that he had reached the end. Roscoe put the hearse in gear and drove out of the cemetery, slowly to give Max once more chance to fade.

But Max wasn't ready for any such thing. He went on moaning. "Those poor fools! None of them know I'm just a cheater, a fraud."

"What?" Roscoe slammed on the brakes. Max flew through the windshield and then drifted back inside and resumed his forlorn position. Roscoe waited for him to explain, but Max had gone silent again. Roscoe restarted the engine and continued down the road. "Listen, Mayor, you built the town library and the bike path and that playground on the south side of the park. Don't you think that's enough?"

"You're too young to remember that flood back in '82, but it wiped out all of Main Street. You might recall lots of folks moved out instead of rebuilding."

"I heard stories." Roscoe merged into the traffic on the highway back to town. "Isn't that when you were elected mayor the first time? I heard you helped out a lot with rebuilding the whole downtown."

"That's what most folks think. But, the truth is I cheated them all. I used aid money to build my own house and buy up all the abandoned and condemned property for myself. I grew rich on the town's misfortune."

So there it was, Max's confession. A lot of folks had done the same--built themselves up on the backs of others and then felt guilty later on. Now that he had told, Roscoe expected Max would fade away.

They turned into the funeral home parking lot, but Max stayed firmly in the front seat.

"It's too late to change anything," Roscoe said. He was beginning to worry about this guy. Already the red carnation was wilting. Folks who stayed around too long could get caught with their spirits floating aimlessly and their forms gradually shredding into pale shrouds. Better to fade, Roscoe thought, better than getting stuck. He stopped the car and looked Max straight on, something he rarely did with ephemerals. "You can't do any more," he said firmly. "Let go."

"Maybe you're right. Maybe I can't." Max's eyes gleamed."But you can."

Glumly, Roscoe shook his head. "Me? I'm not good for much of anything. No one pays attention to me." He pulled up the hood of his jacket and stepped out into the rain, leaving Max in the front seat.

Roscoe lived in a small, efficiency apartment on the third floor of a rundown housing project two blocks from the funeral home. He was dripping by the time he turned the key in the lock and walked in.

Max sat at the kitchen table. "You look like you need a hot cup of coffee, boy."

Without answering, Roscoe took off his wet jacket and hung it on the hook by the door. He filled a mug with hot water and put it in the microwave, then got out a packet of hot chocolate. When the microwave dinged, he poured the hot chocolate mix into the water, and finally sat down opposite Max. "Look, Mayor," he said, sipping gingerly at the steaming liquid. "I told you I'm not the guy to help you out. Everybody already thinks I'm a crazy screwball. No one listens to me."

"Don't worry. I got it all figured out. Say, can you make a cup of that for me?"

"No. You can't drink anything once you're dead. I'll bet you're not cold either."

Max sighed. "Never mind that. Just listen. I got it all figured out what we're going to do."

"I'm not going to speak bad of the dead, even if it would make you feel better." Roscoe sat back in his chair, arms folded firmly across his chest. "It's not fair to talk about folks that can't answer back. And I'm not going to go out and tell all your secrets to the world either. They'd put me in the looney bin."

"You won't have to do any of that." Max drifted over to the stove and hovered above it. "See, I got an idea."

It turned out Max had a whole plan. He thought he could make it up to the town with a big party, dish out hot dogs and ice-cream for everyone and top it all off with a huge display of fireworks. "Everybody gets a little something special that way," he explained. "I always meant to do it, but kept putting it off."

Roscoe tested his hot chocolate and blew on it again. "I haven't got enough money to put on a party for you and me, let alone the whole town."

"But I do." Grinning like a Cheshire cat Max floated up near the ceiling,

"Dead guys don't have anything," Roscoe said. He hated reminding people they were dead, but Max was positively dense on the subject. Roscoe turned out the light and went in the living room to watch TV.

In the morning, Max was in the hearse when Roscoe got to work. The red carnation drooped like a wet rag and Max's clothes looked slept in, though Roscoe knew ephemerals didn't really sleep. There weren't any funerals that day, but Roscoe had to clean, wax and polish the vehicle. Max offered endless advice while Roscoe worked. At first it was nice to have some company. Roscoe usually worked alone, and he really didn't have any friends. But after a while he grew tired of Max's suggestions. Max had a lot more criticism than praise. He kept nagging at Roscoe to hurry up so he could help Max. After three hours, Roscoe would have strangled the guy, if he weren't already dead.

At lunch break, Roscoe declared, "Listen, I'm not robbing your house. All your stuff belongs to your daughters now. I'm not going to jail just to satisfy you."

"You won't have to," Max said.

Roscoe slammed the door on him, not caring that the force

scattered him. It also kept him quiet for almost an hour.

For the next week, Max haunted Roscoe. He would be sitting on Roscoe's chest when he opened his eyes in the morning, and floated between him and the mirror while Roscoe tried to shave.

"It's not stealing," Max said too many times to count. "How can it be stealing if it's my own money? Besides, it's hidden where they'll never find it. If you don't help me, the money will just rot, and nobody will get it."

Roscoe tried driving out to the cemetery three times without telling his boss, just to see if Max would consent to stay there. But Max was stubborn, and Roscoe kept his garrulous shadow.

On Saturday, Max rode along in the hearse for the funeral of Betsy Tillington. By now his skin sagged and his lips were shrinking. When the timid old lady in the coffin tried to whisper a last confession, Max grinned at her. She shrieked, swirled around the back of the hearse, and faded before she could finish her sentence.

"All right. All right" Roscoe threw up his hands in defeat. "What do you want me to do?"

Roscoe wasn't thrilled with Max's plan. He didn't want to be caught breaking and entering, and no matter what Max said, he was the one taking the risk. "Can't we just tell your daughters where the money is, and have them throw a party?"

Max shook his head. "Can't let anybody know it's from me," he said. "Then they'd all know I cheated them. My daughters are proud of me right now. I'd like to keep it that way."

Late that night Roscoe left his apartment dressed in black trousers and a black turtleneck. He felt like he was dressing up for Halloween, and the wispy figure of Max floating just above his left shoulder added to the creepy feeling. Fortunately the street was empty, and Roscoe found his way to the former mayor's yard. The big house was empty, with a 'FOR SALE ' sign on the front lawn. Following Max's whispered instructions, Roscoe snuck around to the back. The rusty gate squeaked on its hinges, and a dog down the street barked. Roscoe's palms were damp with sweat. Tentatively, he shone the flashlight over the yard, then switched it off and sprinted over to the shed. The door was unlocked, but stuck when Roscoe pulled on the knob.

"Pull harder," Max urged. "It's just the damp."

Roscoe yanked the door and it flew open. A stack of flowerpots tipped over and crashed on the cement floor. Lights in the house next door blinked on. Roscoe froze, his heart pounding.

The neighbor walked out to the sidewalk, looking up and down the street, but didn't come into the yard. Apparently satisfied, he went back inside and switched off the light.

"You could be a little quieter," Max said. "I thought you didn't want anyone to hear you."

Roscoe ignored him, and let his eyes adjust to the dim interior of the shed. He picked his way over the broken flowerpots to an old grain bin by the back wall. After brushing away the spider webs, Roscoe raised the heavy lid of the grain bin and took out a stack of moldy burlap sacks. Underneath was a metal chest with a lock. Roscoe lifted it out. Max told him the combination. Roscoe blew off the dust and opened it. Inside, just as Max had promised was a stack of bonds.

The party was held two weeks later at the park beside the cemetery, credited to an anonymous donor, a mystery that had the whole town buzzing with delighted gossip. Everyone came. The rotary club grilled hot dogs and scouts ran the lemonade stand. The park recreation department even set up softball games and 3-legged races.

Max sat beside Roscoe on the bench overlooking the park as the first fireworks lit up the sky.

"There you are," Roscoe said. "You gave the town its party."

"My money," Max said, "but you're the one that made it happen. You whispered in the right ears, sent the bonds to the right people. You organized the whole thing, and you kept my name out of it."

"I guess I did," Roscoe said. He felt six inches taller and good enough to shout. This was the biggest thing he'd ever managed to finish. Then another thought troubled him. "Of course, no one will ever know."

"You'll know," Max said. He stuck out his bony hand. "See you around," he said, fading even as Roscoe took hold to shake it.

The next week Roscoe quit his job driving the hearse and took a position as grounds keeper of the cemetery. Just could be other folks stuck hanging around. They would need helping out, and he was the one for the job.

CONTRIBUTERS

Kayla Fayerweather recently graduated from Winona State University with a B.A. in studio art and minors in art history, arts administration, and English. She currently lives in Utah, surrounded by the Rocky Mountains. Kayla is an aspiring artist and illustrator who loves working with traditional media including pencil, ink, and watercolor. Her other hobbies include reading, exercising, horseback riding, playing games, and hanging out with her cat, Rocky.

David R Greyson is a martial art instructor who claims his hometown is Marion, Ohio. Besides writing and martial arts, he spends his free time pursuing his other passions- photography, sightseeing, and anything that relates to the great outdoors, such as cross-country hiking and kayaking. Having spent more than a decade living in England, he explores as much of Britain as he can. He currently resides in Taunton, Somerset with his faithful dog, Kuro.

Hannah Jones grew up in Eagan, Minnesota. She spent her childhood hating ghost stories. Eventually, however, she came to love them. After graduating from Winona State University with a degree in English and a minor in Chinese, she hopes to go into journalism. Both her articles and her short stories have been published in the *Winona Daily News*. When she's not writing, she's usually reading, drawing, cooking, or jogging.

Teacher, writer, editor, **Terri Evert Karsten** divides her free time between writing books, baking bread and chasing the outdoor life. Terri has been published in *Highlights for Children*,

An Encyclopedia of Women's History and *Rattlesnake Valley Sampler* along with two books, *From Brick to Bread: Building a backyard overn* and *Snags and Sawyers: 2000 Miles Down the Arkansas River.* Her story, *Who's Afraid of the Dark*, was originally published in French under the title *Qui a Peur de l'ombre?* in *Bifurcations*. This translation was first published in the Winona Daily News. Look for Terri on Facebook, or on the Wagonbridge Publishing Website: www.wagonpublishing.com.

Sean Krage has been writing short stories and poems casually for three years. This is his first publised piece. He is currently enrolled at WSU majoring in Theatre and minoring in Creative Writing. For inspiration for both the stage and fiction, Sean listens to a variety of musicians, such as Max Richter and David Helpling, and watches as many movies as he has time for.

Paul Maitrejean grew up in rural Wisconsin, listening to local legend and lore. He published *Devil's Creek* as an ebook in 2011. He currently lives near Tomah, Wisconsin with his wife and three children.

Through the eyes of **N. R. Mehlhoff,** stories are an exploration of life and life is nothing but art. A young man trying his hand in every major creative writing form, Mehlhoff most recently set out to walk 2,500 miles across the U.S. in an attempt to tell a story while telling others' stories. The adventure came to an early halt and is prolonged, but he succeeded in telling a story via blogging and hopes to one day set out again. At this time, he works on a ranch in Colorado writing away, turning ink into a story. You can read Mehlhoff's story of travel on foot at SeeingItSlowly.com

John Michaels is a long time resident of Winona, Minnesota. While he dabbles in everything, he is expert at nothing. *A Night of Storm and Shadow* is his first published writing.

Jordan Elizabeth Mierek is published in *Short Story Me*, *Danse Macabre, Bewildering Stories, Writing Raw, Dark and Dreary Magazine, Storyhouse, the Magical Library, RiverSedge*, and *AboutTeens*. Her work has won awards in The XPress and Utica Writers Club, and she writes for *New Hartford Life magazine*. She is the current president of the Utica Writers Club and has her Bachelor's degree in elementary education. Other stories are available on her WattPad page, http://wattpad.com/JordanMierek, and she keeps a blog about books, writing, and life (because hey, books and writing are her life) at http://kissedbyliterature.blogspot.com/. When not conjuring short stories or nonfiction articles, Jordan enjoys penning novels, and is represented by the Belcastro Agency. Look for Jordan on Facebook – she would love to hear what you think of her stories!

Jeremy Mortis has been writing for several years. *Simon and the ghost* is his first published work. He is a member of the Utica Writers Club and has done a little bit of everything, from playing a mall Santa at Christmas to being a hospital cook. Look for Jeremy on Facebook.

www.ingramcontent.com/pod-product-compliance
Lightning Source LLC
Chambersburg PA
CBHW051847170626
46807CB00003B/1386